CAPE CHARLES IN CRIMSON

A BRANDON HALL MYSTERY 5

JOHN THEO JR.

Cape Charles in Crimson
Paperback Edition

CKN Christian Publishing
An Imprint of Wolfpack Publishing
9850 S. Maryland Parkway, Suite A-5 #323
Las Vegas, Nevada 89183

cknchristianpublishing.com

This book is a work of fiction. Any references to historical events, real people or real places are used fictitiously. Other names, characters, places and events are products of the author's imagination, and any resemblance to actual events, places or persons, living or dead, is entirely coincidental.

eBook ISBN: 978-1-63977-116-5
Paperback ISBN: 978-1-63977-117-2
LCCN: 2022949495

For the beautiful lady who defied odds and lived to the ripe old age of 246. I pray she sees the sun rise on another bicentennial and beyond.

Special thanks to Jim Prendergast and Jason Holmes for their support and input.

CAPE CHARLES IN CRIMSON

God doesn't always respond quickly, but He does act suddenly.

Author Unknown

ONE

The Crossing of the Dan River was a massive part of the Revolutionary War. It happened in South Boston, Virginia, on Valentine's Day in 1781. Unlike the Crossing of the Delaware River, which has been depicted in art, literature, and movies, the Crossing of the Dan was all but lost to history. The Delaware River crossing received far more notoriety for several reasons. It was an offensive led by General Washington himself, and it happened on Christmas night in 1776 when the Continental Army surprised Hessian troops in Trenton, New Jersey. This victorious battle was considered a major turning point in the Revolutionary War. The Crossing of the Dan River, however, was a retreat under lesser-known General Nathanael Greene, but just as important. It occurred during the final months of the War and allowed the Continental Army to escape from the British troops. This indirectly led to the final victory later that year in Yorktown, Virginia.

* * *

A TRACTOR-TRAILER CARRYING lumber rumbled over Tucker C Watkins Memorial Bridge, which snapped me from the eighteenth century back to the twenty-first. I sat on the floating temporary platform in the middle of the Dan River with half my scuba gear on and my feet dangling in the muddy water. The lady beside me was fresh out of grad school with a Ph.D. in archaeology from VCU. Her name was Sandra Scott. She was around thirty, a short, plump woman who ordered people around like they were children at a playground. Dr. Scott received a grant to create a cofferdam and temporarily redirect part of the river around the location where part of the historical Crossing of the Dan occurred back in 1781. Based on her academic research, Dr. Scott discovered a lost letter from General Greene to the Continental Congress. In this letter, General Greene explained how a single float of supplies broke free during the crossing and sank. According to Greene's manifest, on the boat were two cannons, two barrels of powder, shot, and one bag of gold set aside to pay the soldiers who were fed up with the worthless Continental currency. Dr. Scott pitched the idea to redirect, drain, and dredge a small portion of the Dan River to search for the lost items.

"Mr. Hall, we're working on a timetable here."

I finished putting the hood up on the wetsuit. "I'm almost ready, Dr. Spock."

Dr. Spock was the nickname I called Dr. Scott as she seemed to be all logic, like the Vulcan from *Star Trek,* and like the aforementioned Vulcan, showed very little emotion. However, when I called her Spock, she would reveal what some would consider a grin. I seemed to be the only one who could get away with it. The first day Dr. Scott showed up on the job, one of the construction guys made the mistake of calling her sweetie. Within minutes she established her alpha-femaleness by assaulting them with a level of verbal acumen that went well over everyone's heads. By the end of that day, everyone called her Dr. Scott, ma'am, or boss lady. That was a week ago. Since then, she had eased up a bit, but was still all business.

I lowered my mask, stuck the regulator in my mouth, and flopped backward off the platform into the water. Immediately, the rush of the river pulled tight against the safety line that kept me from being washed downstream. The Dan River water table was low from the summer drought, but the water still moved at over three knots. The three-millimeter wetsuit I wore was enough to keep me warm in the cool water. I had only been in this part of the Dan River two other times when drunk drivers barreled off Watkins Bridge. It was a nasty section of the river, which eventually found its way into Buggs Island Lake in Clarksville. Visibility was nil in the muddy water. I let air out of my buoyancy control device, or BCD, and pulled hand over hand on the rope to the bottom. This is where the cofferdam, made up of steel sheet piles, would be placed. This circular metal structure would be driven into the riverbed, and the water inside the self-contained space pumped out, allowing archaeological work to commence on a section of dry riverbed.

Tethered to my back was the metal detector sonar device I would run over the bottom, which relayed signals to a laptop Dr. Scott monitored topside. So far, we had found a lot of buried items that showed up as metal. Cans, parts of automobiles, and a grocery cart, but two items took the rough shape of cannons that lay side by side in the mud buried fifteen feet beneath me. I was doing a final scan to make sure the cofferdam would go in the right location. The last thing we needed was to redirect the river and find out we needed the cofferdam to be another five feet downstream. I tethered myself into another line anchored into the bottom and kept moving. After thirty minutes of pulling myself back and forth in a grid-like pattern, I went topside.

Dr. Scott found me on the platform removing my mask and tank. "That should do it, Mr. Hall."

"Need me for anything else?"

"Construction crew will take over from here. You can collect your check from the foreman on your way out."

"I wish you the best," I said. "I'm excited to see what you find."

"I'm cautiously optimistic," she said. "This could be one of the biggest Revolutionary War discoveries in the last hundred years."

"You'll be famous overnight and go on a speaking circuit," I said. "Then write a New York Times bestseller, wear sunglasses when its cloudy, and—"

"Oh, shut up," she said.

"Take care, Dr. Spock."

I picked up the check and loaded my scuba gear into the back of my 1976 F-250. By the time I reached the bank in downtown South Boston, my hair was dry, and the late morning temperature had just topped ninety. After cashing the check, I headed north toward Nathalie, which was home. The cash in my shirt pocket was enough to cover our upcoming vacation as well as a few other unforeseen expenses that crept up on us.

Five minutes into the drive, I noticed a pickup truck behind me. It was a new white pickup converted into a lowrider, a trend where the owner lowered the suspension to make it look like a hot rod. It was usually done to old 1960s trucks, giving them almost no ground clearance, but this was a brand-new truck, which I had never seen done before. There was nothing pragmatic about doing this modification to a new pickup, and it made the four-wheel drive completely useless due to the street tires and zero ground clearance.

The truck followed me through South Boston into downtown Halifax and along Route 501 for quite a distance. There was a very good chance the driver was a college kid heading up to Lynchburg, but after the experiences I had over the past few years, my internal radar was on alert.

I dialed my buddy Tollers who was a sheriff. He picked up on the first ring. "Don't tell me," he said. "You're gonna bail on vacation?"

"I'm still going," I said. "I need a favor. There's a brand-new lowrider truck that's been following me since I left downtown Sobo. Can you run a plate for me?"

"Hold on a minute and I'll pull over so I can access my onboard computer. Man, why do these young kids take a perfectly functional truck and deliberately handicap it?"

"No idea," I said.

"Okay, go."

I put the phone on speaker and looked in the rearview mirror. "Okay, it's a North Carolina plate. Victor, Alpha, Charlie, one, three, three, five."

There was a long pause before Tollers said, "Belongs to a Richard Stanwick, twenty-three. Looks like he just moved to Roxboro. Clean record. Name ring a bell?"

"No," I said. "Maybe just a coincidence. A lot of people take this route."

"Doubtful with your track record," Tollers laughed.

"Text me if you need anything done at the farm while you're gone."

"Roger that, and thanks."

Just before I turned off Route 501 onto Bradley Creek Road, the truck continued on 501. Ten minutes later, I pulled into our 500-acre farm. We named the farm Twenty-Three-One, after the Psalm of the same number. *The Lord is my shepherd, I shall not want.* It was nice to see cattle flourishing in the main pasture once again. There had been a time when we lost the entire herd, and almost the farm itself. Like the Psalm mentioned, the Lord had been faithful.

Parked in front of our farmhouse was an older Chinook Concourse recreational vehicle. A twenty-one-foot class B+ RV that was going to be our road trip vehicle of choice for this vacation. My tween daughter, Emily, was in the process of loading up the vehicle and waved as I drove toward the barn to park. Inside the barn was a large central workspace. There were a few horse stalls I had repurposed into a small gym, and an office. At the far end was a door to the barn apartment. Before I could knock, Amber Schilling opened the door. The twenty-year-old was dressed in sweats with a hanky covering her auburn hair. Her tan face and clothes were sprinkled with white speckles of paint.

"Brandon, I'm just cleaning up. Shut your eyes and take one step forward."

Amber had legally become part of our family in recent months. She had lost her brother a few years ago in a local race car crash. Then both her father, a famous Virginia Senator, along with her mother, died within a week of each other in tragically different ways. I had worked for her father on two occasions, and my wife and I decided to take Amber in. We cared for her as best we could through her trauma, depression, and anxiety. By God's grace, she made it through. However, she was still not a hundred percent recovered.

My daughter, Emily, had grown to love Amber like an older sister, and we decided to offer her our home as an anchor point and made the unorthodox move to adopt a nearly grown woman, which seemed to be the final medicine in her recovery. Amber had moved into the small vacant barn apartment, and when we refused to charge her rent, she insisted on remodeling the place. Once we finished all the rough work, like plumbing and electric, Amber took over and banished me until the place was finished. Today was the big reveal.

"I've been dying to see the place," I said, stepping inside.

"Okay, open your eyes," Amber said.

The small apartment looked stunning, like it was from a magazine photo spread. White shiplap lined almost every wall. The small kitchenette counters were soapstone offset with cherry cabinets. In the living room, a white couch and loveseat sat on refinished, original, wide-oak floors. She had blasted through the ceiling and recaptured the entire height of the barn's thirty-plus-foot height. Ascending windows allowed daylight to wash down into the apartment. A small woodstove sat in the corner of the living room to finish the country-cozy motif.

"Amber, I'm at a loss for words," I said. "The place is stunning. I love that you kept the original floors. And the cherry cabinets against the shiplap and counter look incredible. Oh no."

"What's wrong?" she gasped.

"When Annie sees this, she's going to make me redo our entire house now."

Amber laughed. "Don't scare me like that! Now, come see the rest of the apartment."

The bathroom had a clawfoot tub and rain showerhead, and the bedroom was simple yet bright.

I kept repeating the word "Stunning" as I wandered back into the kitchenette. "Mind if I get a cup of water?"

"Go ahead," she said. "The second faucet next to the sink makes soda water if you want."

"Fancy," I said, filling up a plastic cup. On the counter was her smartphone. I saw close to a dozen missed calls from a single phone number with a 336 area code. It was a North Carolina number. "Someone's been trying to call you."

"Huh? Oh, that's just my cousin's employee."

"You mean Cousin Ricky? The guy who showed up here before?" I said, remembering my encounter with her snobbishly rude cousin from North Carolina, which almost ended in a fistfight.

"The one and only."

"If you don't mind me asking, why's this guy calling you one… two… three… ten times?"

"He's hired muscle for my cousin," Amber said, adjusting a pillow on her couch. "Do you think I should swap the loveseat and couch?"

"He's what?" I said. "Back up a minute. Just what is it that your cousin Ricky does for a living?"

"He's a lawyer, but his family also owns apartments in North Carolina as well as a recycling plant."

"Those don't sound like shady businesses to me," I said.

"The apartments are legit, even though he's a slumlord. The recycling plant my dad believed was the shady business."

"Like?"

"Not sure. Historically trash companies in the northeast were notorious for being fronts for the mafia."

"Is that why he needs hired muscle?

"Probably."

"What's this guy's name?"

"He goes by Romeo," she laughed. "Thinks he's a ladies' man or something, but I think his name's Stanwich or Stinewick or—"

"Stanwick?"

"Yeah," she said. "How'd you know?

"Lucky guess," I said.

"Seriously, Brandon?"

"If he's the same Stanwick who drives a brand-new white lowrider pickup, then he was just trailing me on 501."

Amber didn't say anything, so I moved the conversation along. "Why's he calling you, and why haven't you told me any of this?"

"Cousin Ricky's struggling financially," she said. "He's got a gambling problem, along with five kids from two ex-wives and an ex-girlfriend."

I tried to do the math on my fingers of wives and girlfriends versus kid ratio.

"He's trying to find a way into my inheritance. I'm worth over $50 million you know."

I dropped my cup of water on the floor. Amber laughed so hard she snorted.

"I'm sorry," I said, reaching for an embroidered towel from the oven handle.

"It would have been more," Amber continued, "but Daddy's suicide nullified his insurance policies, so I only got the family inheritance and Mom's policy."

I returned to the sink with the wet towel and refilled

my cup with water. "That's a big enough nest egg to let you do whatever you want with your life."

"I think I like the couch and loveseat where they are," she said.

"I agree," I said. "But can we talk about your cousin and his muscle for a minute?"

"I can handle them."

"But—"

"Don't worry about it, Brandon. I still have contact with Dad's lawyers, and I'm not some naive little girl, you know."

"I know, but with that much money, you're gonna have a target on your back and—"

"Don't worry," Amber said, folding a blanket and laying it perfectly on the corner of the couch. "By the way, I listed you and Annie as my beneficiaries."

I spat out the refilled water and proceeded into a coughing fit. I hunched over, and Amber came up behind me and started to slap my back. I held up my hand for her to stop.

"Are you okay?"

I shook my head back and forth as if to say, *give me a minute*. When I cleared my throat, I asked, "Are you crazy?"

"That's a rude thing to say to someone who struggles with anxiety."

"Sorry, but are you insane?" I repeated in the same tone.

"That's even worse," she said, trying not to laugh.

She dropped this on me for shock value, or to test me, like her dad used to do. "You know what I mean, Amber."

"You and Annie have welcomed me into this family and haven't even charged me rent." She pursed her lips and shrugged her shoulders. "I guess we're family in name only, and you guys never really meant any of it. Blood is thicker than water, as they say."

I laughed, which started me coughing again. Once I regained my composure, I said, "You are your father's daughter. A master of mind games and manipulation."

"Thank you," she said. "I'll take that as a compliment. Besides, who else should I list as a beneficiary? Cousin Ricky?"

"Well, no," I said, thinking as quickly as possible. "You're gonna have a family one day, right?"

"Last time I checked, I don't have a husband or children." She said with a victorious smirk. "When I do, I'll change the policy."

Annie came into the apartment and found me still hunched over. "Are you okay?"

"Yeah, water just went down the wrong pipe," I said, finally standing up. "Our newest family member has somehow given me her panic attacks."

"What do you mean?" Annie said, turning to Amber.

"Your husband is being oh-so melodramatic," Amber said, continuing to adjust pillows on the couch.

Annie looked confused.

"Never mind," I said.

Amber gave Annie the tour of the finished apartment, and her responses were as awestruck as mine. "Brandon, this has inspired me to redo our living room and kitchen."

"See, Amber," I mock huffed. "You threw me under the bus."

* * *

OUTSIDE, in the main pasture, Dad was on the back of his horse, Savannah. Even wearing a baseball cap, he still looked like John Wayne whenever he was on horseback. Probably because he was over six feet and still maintained his marine workout of daily runs, pushups, pull-ups, and sit-ups. Dad had a lariat out and used the loop to nudge a few heifers along. Mom stood by the fence, shouting at him to come take a bottle of water. Dad either didn't hear or ignored her.

I avoided the argument and headed back toward our farmhouse. Emily played under an oak tree with our infant daughter, Addison.

"All packed?" I said.

"All set," Emily said. "I'm so excited. Can we please get on the road?"

"Let me just grab my stuff."

My cell phone rang just as I entered the side door into the kitchen. "Brandon Hall speaking?"

"How's my favorite employee doing?" Roger Drake said.

Roger was my clandestine friend from the DC area who hired me from time to time for contract work. "I'm taking the family on a much-needed vacation to the beach."

"Where to?"

"Eastern Shore," I said. "Cape Charles, to be specific. And no, I'm not available for the next week."

"The world's a mess, my brother," Drake said. "Russia's doing exercises off the coast of Hawaii as if to taunt us, China's saber-rattling around Taiwan, our country is a wreck under this new administration."

"I don't even want to know what the job entails," I said.

"All I can say is it has to do with Space Force and Antarctica."

"Boring is my new favorite word, Roger." I changed the subject before he could pitch me from another angle. "How's Vanessa and your granddaughter?"

"Vanessa will never be the same since Jae passed," he said, referring to his son-in-law, who died on one of our missions. "But Rachel has brought a much-needed light back into the Drake family."

"Vanessa ever coming back to work for you?"

"She's content being a full-time mother for now."

"And Homer, Paronto, and Bridgett?" I said, referring to his new team.

"They're all doing well. Homer's son is adorable. Little Johnny, but we're calling him Little Hoss per Homer's instructions."

"How are you holding up under this hostile administration in DC?"

"We're lying low and just biding our time," he said. "During the chaos of recent elections, I had the foresight to place my group under SOCOM, so we've all but disappeared. You sure I can't convince you—"

"I'm sure," I said.

"You getting fat and happy with those government paychecks I got you?"

"No, I just really want a vacation, and so does my wife. We got a great deal on a small guesthouse in Cape Charles, and I'm not passing it up."

"I just can't picture you wearing those beat-up cowboy boots, a speedo, tank top, and sunglasses, my friend."

I had to laugh at the image. "I'm not all country boy, you know."

"You're not the relaxing type, Brandon."

"I have a couple of magazines, my saltwater fishing rod, and scuba gear in case I get adventurous. I aim to relax as much as possible."

"Okay, well, you know I'm just pushing your buttons. Enjoy the much-deserved time off, my brother. Be thinking of us freezing our butts off while you're on the beach with your lovely family. "

TWO

The Chinook RV was a loaner from Tollers. It was big enough for two people to sleep in overnight, but we were just using it for the road trip. Amber still did not like to travel far from home. I figured the RV had a kitchenette, refrigerator, full bathroom, couch, and television, which would help her relax in case her anxiety spiked on the road trip. Inside, Emily and Amber sat in swivel chairs facing one another over a dinette table playing Uno.

"Are we leaving?" Emily said, tossing down a pair of cards.

"In a minute," I said, making sure the baby's car seat was secured on the couch across from them.

Annie stepped inside carrying Addison. She wore a pretty sundress with her brunette hair tucked under a sun hat, as well as her new sunglasses, which I had to convince her it was okay to purchase. "We all set?"

"Emily, you didn't tell me we were bringing along a twenty-five-year-old nanny?"

"Huh?"

"Never mind, that's your momma who just stepped on board?"

"That's so cheesy," Amber said.

"Oh, shush," Annie said, placing Addison in the car seat.

"Everyone all set?"

"Yes," came the group answer.

"I'm gonna do a final walk through the house, and then we can head out." I stepped through the rear exit of the RV and went inside the house. The light timers were set, all the windows were locked, and the water valves to the washing machine were shut off. Mom would collect our mail, and Dad would keep an eye on all other farm-related items.

Outside, Dad rode up on horseback to the closest fence line to meet me. "Have fun and watch out for weirdos."

"You sure you can handle this place alone, old man?"

He laughed and turned the horse back toward the pasture and galloped off at a pace faster than a man his age should ride. Inside the RV, we said a quick prayer for safe travels and were off. We had around a four-hour trip ahead of us to the Eastern Shore of Virginia.

"Tell me about this place you've rented again?" Annie said.

"It's a two-bedroom guesthouse on a farm just outside of Cape Charles."

"And you met this guy on your last contract job working for Roger?"

"Yeah, I stayed overnight," I said. "It's nothing fancy, but the house is big enough and—" I lowered my voice down to a whisper, "I got a great deal on it."

"What do you mean by nothing fancy?" Annie said, a look of concern across her face.

"It's a dated two-bedroom guesthouse, but everything else is booked in Cape Charles into October."

"I'm fine with dated," Annie said. "I just hope it's clean."

"I'm pretty sure it was clean," I said, trying to remember if it was clean from the brief time I spent there. "Worst case, we can shack up in the RV if you don't like it."

"For some alone time and romance," Amber giggled from behind us at the dinette.

"And smoochie time," Emily added.

"Girls!" Annie blushed.

"Oh, Mom," Emily said, "I'm not naive, but that is disgusting." She threw down a pair of cards. "Uno!"

"There's Addison's innocent ears," I said, reaching across for Annie's hand. "Still, sweetie, maybe we could sneak off—"

"Brandon!"

* * *

TRAFFIC WAS smooth until we hit the coast. After sitting in traffic on the Chesapeake Bay Bridge for forty minutes, we inched our way into Cape Charles and pulled into Luke Seabold's farm. The last time I had been there, it had been a dreary fall day, and every living thing seemed to be dead. From trees to the farm crop. Today, healthy corn stalks stretched as far as the eye could see. An antique yellow biplane flew overhead, and a John Deere tractor from the 1960s sat outside his small farmhouse. It looked like a movie set from an old Frank Capra film. I pulled up in front of the guesthouse and parked. As soon as I shut off the RV, the girls rushed into the guesthouse. Annie followed while I carried in Addison, who was asleep. The inside of the guesthouse was the same way I remembered it. Clean, but dated from the sixties with laminate counters and salmon-colored appliances. The kitchen flowed into a small living room. There were two bedrooms and a small bathroom

"Well, it could be worse," Annie said, walking out of the master bedroom and into the guest room where two twin beds were set up. "The girls can sleep in here, and we can set up the pack 'n play in the living room for Addison to sleep in."

"It's just a place to crash at night," I said. "Hopefully, we'll be at the beach the rest of the time."

Amber came out of the guest room, and I couldn't read her expression. "Not what you're used to, huh?"

She grinned. "It's perfect."

"Really? Not too lowbrow for the boarding schools and brownstones you're used to?"

"The last thing I want to see are cold, unlived-in mansions. I like being in a small house with the people I love. The cozier, the better."

Hearing that made my heart swell. "Well, this is as cozy as it gets."

Annie started to change Addison on the couch, but Amber took over. "Here, let me do that while you unpack."

While everyone got settled, I walked the short distance over to the main farmhouse. I knocked on the side door, but no one answered. Overhead, the yellow biplane circled. After about a minute, it landed on a grassed area somewhere behind a large red barn out back. I walked out to see if the pilot turned out to be my friend. Sure enough, Luke Seabold stepped from the open cockpit with goggles on top of his head. The old man climbed down the wing and plopped on the ground like someone in their twenties.

"You're a man with many talents," I said, shaking his hand.

"Hate dusting the crops with anything, but I do use organic compounds," he said.

"I paid a guy to seed a couple of pastures by plane last year," I said. "If only our great-granddaddies could see us now."

"I know," Luke said. "You guys find everything you need in the guesthouse?"

"Yes, sir," I said, handing him an envelope with cash. "I appreciate the deal you gave me on the place. I know it's the height of summer, and rentals are going for top dollar."

The old man shrugged his shoulders and put the envelope in his shirt pocket. "You get the family-and-friends discount."

"Aren't you gonna count the money?"

Luke waived his hand as if I'd asked a silly question. "Can I interest you in a cup of sweet tea?"

"I think the kids and my wife are itching to get their toes in the water. Can I take a rain check?"

"Sure thing," he said. "Let me know if you need anything."

* * *

A SHORT WHILE LATER, we drove through downtown Cape Charles. The main road was Mason Avenue, which was a hive of activity. Flip-flop-clad patrons came and went from cute gift shops and restaurants. We parked along Bay Avenue and found our way onto the beach via a boardwalk that wound through dunes and salt marsh grass. I made several trips back to the RV to bring out the blankets, chairs, and toys. By the time I finished, Amber and Emily had already dunked in the water, and Annie was waist-deep holding Addison.

"Our baby's first taste of the ocean," Annie said.

"You didn't wait for me," I said, dropping the blankets and toys to snap a picture with my cell phone.

As I set up the umbrella, Annie called from the water. "Get in here. It's like bathwater."

"I'll be right in."

"I'm glad you stumbled on this town," she said. "I can't believe we've never been here before."

"I knew you'd love it."

A half-hour later, Annie and I relaxed in beach chairs while Amber and Emily played on a blanket with Addison. Overhead, the sun blazed in a cloudless sky, and the temperature was just south of ninety, but a nice breeze kept it comfortable. A small radio Annie had brought played the local news. I exhaled as if I had been holding my breath for years. I could finally relax. I leaned back in the beach chair and shut my eyes.

The static of the radio increased, and I instinctively moved the antennae a bit. The signal crystalized as the announcer was in the middle of an urgent update. "First ever recorded shark attack in the Chesapeake Bay. The scuba diver was a twenty-six-year-old male. He was bitten just off of Tangier Lighthouse. The diver was medevac'd from Tangier Island to Sentara General Hospital in Virginia Beach. He is in a stable condition, and no other details are known at this time."

"Great," Annie said. "We just got here and now have to worry about shark attacks?"

I looked up on my cell phone where Tangier Lighthouse was. "Sweetie, the attack was nowhere near here, it was way up the Chesapeake Bay. I wouldn't worry about it."

"I'm not going back in that water," Amber said. "I got enough anxiety on my plate."

Emily turned to me, her dark eyes wide. "Daddy?"

"You're more likely to be struck by lightning than bitten by a shark," I said.

"Tell that to the scuba diver getting stitched up in Virginia Beach," Amber said, handing Addison over to Emily.

Emily's wet brunette ponytail bobbed back and forth between Amber and me. I didn't want her to be afraid of the water. "I've been scuba diving since my days in the Marines. Hundreds of dives, and I've only seen a couple of small sharks in the wild. They generally leave you alone."

"Unless they're hungry," Amber said.

"That's it," I said, grabbing Amber and hoisting her over my shoulders.

Emily squeaked, "Throw her in. Throw her in!"

Annie took the baby from Emily, "Oh, be careful."

"Don't you dare, Brandon!" Amber shouted.

I walked into waist-high water with Amber kicking and shouting. Emily bounced around me like a little bunny shouting for me to dunk her big sis. Instead, I gently dropped Amber into the waist-deep water.

"See, you're fine," I said. I widened my eyes and pointed behind her. "Oh my gosh! Is that a fin?" I turned and sprinted back toward Annie and Addison, trying not to laugh. Amber and Emily screamed from behind me. They met me on the blanket and proceeded to throw sand all over me.

"Hey, that's mean," I said.

"That's what you deserve," Annie said.

* * *

WE STAYED at the beach for the rest of the afternoon to watch the sunset. Cape Charles faced west, so you were able to see the sun set into the water as if we were on the west coast of the United States. On the drive back to the rental house, we picked up a couple of pizzas and salads from a takeout restaurant. When we pulled up to the guesthouse, Luke waved *hello* to us from the front porch of his farmhouse. He talked with a young brunette girl I recognized from the last time I was there as his granddaughter. I parked the RV and started walking toward them to say hi, but realized they seemed to be in an argument. Instead, I did a quick about-face and went back to the guesthouse. After dinner and showers, the girls found a cabinet full of VHS tapes to go along with an ancient television and VHS player in their bedroom. They picked some black-and-white films to watch from their twin beds with bowls of popcorn. I shut their door and dimmed the lights in the living room as Annie rocked Addison to sleep in a wicker chair.

"I think Amber likes hanging with Emily," I whispered. "It lets her relive the childhood she never had."

Annie added. "I agree. It lets her escape into an innocent bubble."

There was a light knock on the front door. Luke was out front. I stepped outside to talk to him and shut the door behind me. "I'd have you come in," I whispered, "but the wife is putting the baby down."

"Tomorrow, maybe," he said. "Sorry to bother you, but you got a minute?"

"Sure."

The older man started to walk back toward his house, and I followed. The night air was warm and the stars in the sky were shrouded by the light pollution from the highway and stores nearby.

"Everything okay in the guesthouse?"

"Everything's fine," I said. "You have a beautiful property."

"It was better when I was a child and no one cared about going to the beach. There was very little traffic or crowds around here. The people on the coast were mostly poor, but we were left alone." We made our way past a mid-1980s F-150 pickup truck toward his barn, where the nose of the biplane stuck out. "You still doing PI work, Brandon?"

"A bit," I said, knowing that whatever he was going to say next would impact my vacation.

"I could use some help with an issue I'm having."

"Something to do with your granddaughter?"

He stopped and turned to me. "You're good."

"Lucky guess," I said. "What's the problem?"

"For starters, my daughter-in-law is missing."

"Have you notified the police?"

"Yes, but they know her and know her reputation. She's not the real issue, though."

"A missing person isn't a problem?"

"She'll show up eventually," he said, shrugging his shoulders.

"I hate to pry, Luke, but I'd need you to fill in the blanks a bit."

Luke rested his hand on the edge of the barn as if to stabilize himself. "I lost my wife to cancer about twenty years ago. Like Abraham and Sarah, Sue and I struggled until later in life to have a child. We thought we were the most blessed family in the world when Thomas was born. You remind me of Thomas. He also had a beard like yours and was about your build. Maybe that's why I like you."

"I'm assuming that he passed away?"

Luke dropped his head. "Thomas was in Special Forces and died in Afghanistan seventeen years ago. I tried to be there for Marcy and her mom Cassie, but emotional support was my wife's area of expertise."

"What happened?"

"After Thomas's death, Cassie went from a church-going middle-class mother to working for this antique car dealer. The next thing I know, she's got tattoos, smokes like a chimney, and goes missing for days, even weeks."

"How's your granddaughter handling it?"

"Marcy claims her mom has to deliver antique cars to places like Miami, and as far north as Long Island, but she's smart and knows her mother is self-absorbed and spiraling downward—" he paused, as if he were picking his words carefully. "Cassie will sometimes go on a road trip that should only take two or three days and comes back a week later."

"Where does your granddaughter stay when she's away?"

"With me."

"So you want me to look into the mom's disappearance while I'm here?"

"No," Luke said. "Cassie is an adult, but Marcy is the one I'm concerned about. She's become quite a handful, hanging out with a tough crowd and starting to give me an attitude. The group she hangs with gets together behind the strip mall down the street most days and nights with their pickup trucks. Some of us think there are drug deals going on down there. For some reason, the police are aware of them but haven't done anything. I just don't want Marcy getting caught up in anything illegal, but she claims the kids are all just hanging out and playing games and tells me to butt out."

"You think being new in town might allow me the ability to poke around down there and not get noticed."

Luke smiled. "Kind of. The more I try to get involved, the more I seem to drive Marcy toward this group."

"Have you tried to talk to her mom?"

"A couple of times, but Cassie's too self-absorbed in her world. I think she could be hooked on drugs, which is why I'm not surprised she's a few days late in returning."

"So, if I'm understanding this fragile ecosystem correctly," I said. "You want me to check out this group your granddaughter is hanging out with? If they're into something bad, then find dirt on them and maybe present it to the police?" Luke nodded, so I continued. "The group gets bagged and goes away, and you've passively pulled your granddaughter away without lifting a finger, or more important, having her hate you or driving any wedge between the two of you?"

"Boy, you're good," Luke said, a smile replacing his concerned frown. "Have you ever done anything like this before?"

"Once or twice."

"Then you'll help me?"

"I've been looking forward to this vacation, Luke. I haven't taken my wife away in years—"

"Here," he said, removing the envelope of cash I had given him. "I'll give your money back for the week, and I'll even pay you extra."

"It's not the money," I said, raising my hands to refuse

the envelope. I also realized it took a lot for him to ask for help.

"I'll double your normal fee," Luke said.

I knew he wasn't a man of means. "Tell you what," I said. "Hold onto my envelope for now, but I'll poke around and see what I can come up with."

Even in the dimming light, I could see Luke's eyes widen and then immediately start to fill up. "I can't tell you how much I appreciate this, Brandon. I'm going to pay you something for your time."

"You've already given me a deep discount on the guesthouse during the busiest time of the year. And the last time I was here, I brought a load of trouble that caused you enough electrical damage."

"Yeah, but your government friend sent me a check which more than covered the damages, so—"

"Let me poke around and see what I can see. I may not be able to do anything."

"Fair enough," he said.

Back in the guesthouse, Annie was in bed reading a beach romance called *Cape Ann*. "Where were you?"

"Luke, the owner, asked me to do a side job while I'm here."

Annie closed the book. "And you told him absolutely no, right?" I didn't answer, and she repeated. "You did tell him no, Brandon?"

"He's an old widower who's looking after his granddaughter and needs—"

"Oh, you are such a sucker. You can never say no, can you?"

I leaned over and turned the light out. "I can never say no to my gorgeous wife in bed."

"Brandon," Annie lowered her voice. "The kids are right on the other side of this wall."

"Then be quiet," I whispered.

"But Addison could wake up."

"We can always sneak out to the Chinook. If the RV's a rockin', don't come knockin'—"

"Oh, will you stop with that."

THREE

The next morning, we found a coffee shop on Mason Avenue. Emily and I went inside to order while everyone else remained in the RV. The place was busy with families sitting around fancy tables eating meals like French toast and eggs benedict. The smell of rich coffee beans mixed with the breakfast meals made my stomach growl. The interior of the coffee shop looked like it was from the 1920s, with old nautical oil paintings and an ornate tin ceiling. A stairway led up to a bright function room on the second floor. I ordered iced coffees for me and Annie, a smoothie for Emily, and an herbal tea for Amber. While Emily went to use the bathroom, I was left waiting for the order and the next batch of muffins to come out of the oven.

"Muffins will be right out in a minute," the late-thirties man with a dark, upcurled handlebar mustache said. "You on vacation?"

"Yeah, I'm falling in love with your town," I said. "Name's Brandon. You the owner?"

"Will," he said, shaking my hand.

"Your place is gorgeous," I said. "I'm a sucker for old architecture, and your 'stache goes with the motif."

Will chuckled. "The building's got character for sure. Built in 1923."

"Mind if I wander upstairs?"

"Be my guest," he said.

The second floor was a beautiful sunlit function room with scattered wrought iron tables. It looked like it was used for parties or even small wedding receptions. Off to the side, a solitary older man with gray hair, a seersucker blazer, and a peach-colored bow tie sat alone with a cup of tea, a worn Bible, and a leather-bound notebook. He seemed to fit in perfectly with the architecture and era of the coffee shop.

"Nice day we're having," he said in a Cajun accent I placed somewhere in the Gulf Coast part of the country.

"It's perfect out," I said. "I like your bow tie."

"Thank you," he said.

"What chapter are you reading?"

"I was just finishing Malachai," he said, closing the Bible and looking up. "I'm studying stories that involve patience and waiting on the Lord. Did you know there was a four-hundred-year gap between the end of Malachai and the beginning of the New Testament?"

"I do."

"Aha, I could tell right away you were a believer the moment you walked up the stairs."

I laughed. "How can you tell?"

He shrugged his shoulders. "Just a gift I have. Believers stick out to me in crowds." He pointed to my waist. "By the way, you're printing."

"Excuse me?"

"Your gun. It's showing through your shirt."

I pulled up my sagging cargo shorts and adjusted my

shirt to make sure the appendix holster for my nine-millimeter Smith and Wesson was completely concealed. "You're quite the observant fellow," I said.

He reached his hand across the table. His dress shirt had cufflinks with what looked like ancient Greek lettering on them. "Charles Coyne."

"Brandon Hall," I said, taking his hand.

"Are you police, or government?"

"Neither," I said. "I'm just a farmer on vacation."

"You always conceal-carry on vacation?"

"Old habits," I said, starting to become more curious than annoyed at the older man's questions. I respected people who were observant in an age of selfies and cell phones. "What do you do, Charles? Are you a pastor?"

"Retired lawyer."

"You don't miss a thing," I said. "You look like you're dressed to go to an important meeting."

He repeated my response back to me. "Old habits."

Emily came up with the order in hand. "I'm ready whenever you are."

"Charles, this is my daughter, Emily."

He rose from behind the table to stand well over six feet and shook Emily's hand. "Nice to meet you, young lady."

"I like your bow tie," Emily said.

"Like father like daughter," Charles chuckled. "Are you heading to the beach?"

"Plan on spending most of our time there," I said.

"It's a gorgeous part of the country."

"I can tell by your accent that you're not from around here," I said.

"I'm a transplant," he said, pulling out an antique pocket watch and checking the time.

"Well, it was nice to meet you," Emily said, nudging me. "C'mon."

"Nice to meet you as well," Charles said, doing a slight bow.

* * *

WE PARKED at a different spot on Bay Avenue and stayed in the RV to have breakfast. Annie and I turned our chairs around to face Emily and Amber, who sat across from one another at the dinette table, while Addison walked up and down the aisle, dropping more crumbs on the floor than in her mouth.

"This is the way to travel," I said, taking a sip of iced coffee. "We have a virtual apartment with this RV."

"It's so pretty here," Annie said, looking out the window. "There isn't a cloud in the sky, and it's going to be a perfect beach day."

* * *

WE SPENT the day on the beach, only breaking to have lunch in the RV with sandwiches Annie had made. We left the beach before sunset as everyone, except Amber, was starting to sunburn. On the way home, we picked up dinner at a local seafood restaurant. By the time everyone showered, I had dinner set out in the small living room. Two window air conditioners kept the house nice and cool. After dinner, Emily and Amber picked out another VHS movie to watch in their bedroom while Annie played with Addison outside in the small front yard.

"I'm going to the store to get a few items," I said. "We need anything?"

"Why don't you get some organic applesauce for Addison," Annie said.

"Roger that."

* * *

TEN MINUTES LATER, I pulled into the parking lot of the strip mall that housed the local grocery store as well as a hair salon, restaurant, liquor store, and Dollar General store. This was the strip mall Luke said his granddaughter hung out behind. I picked up the applesauce as well as some other snacks, along with spring water. After loading the items into the RV, I walked around the parking lot and found my way out back. Behind the strip mall was a massive parking lot that abutted an old Little League baseball field. The infield dirt was overgrown with weeds. To the far left, tucked against the end of the parking lot where it met a forest, were four fancy, jacked up pickup trucks and several motorcycles. The cheapest truck, I figured, was in the $45,000 range.

Kids hung out in the cabs and beds of the trucks with music blasting that was a mixture of drums, heavy bass, and cuss words. None of the kids seemed older than twenty-one, which told me they were either from rich parents, or were making money far above their experience level to afford those vehicles. Most of the girls wore skimpy shorts and either bikini tops or tight shirts. The guys wore shorts without shirts, or tank tops. A few smoked cigarettes, but I didn't see any alcohol or drugs being used.

On the baseball field, a half dozen young males played a game of whiffle ball, with swearing being the regular form of communication. It didn't look innocent, but it didn't look illegal. I approached the chain-link fence overlooking the ball field and made like I was interested in the whiffle ball game. After a minute, I pretended to text something on my cell phone. I glanced over at the trucks again about twenty-five yards away. A single bottle of alcohol was passed from one truck to another. Bad, but still not in the high-crime realm. I counted nine females and eight males. From what I could, see none of the girls matched Luke's brunette granddaughter. They all saw me, so I couldn't snap any pictures. Beyond the baseball field's third baseline, was a thicket of trees where I could covertly observe the group further the next time I came back. I just needed to find a way to sneak into the woods from a different direction. I turned to leave, and three young white males approached from the direction of the trucks. Their shorts were sagging, and only one of them wore a tank top.

"You lost or something?" one of the skinny white boys said, using his hands to annunciate like he was a gangsta.

"I was just leaving," I said.

The tallest one, who had an impressive upper body physique, smiled. "You're not leaving until I say so."

"I'm sorry I'm not from around here," I said. "I was just watching the whiffle ball game."

"Punk's afraid," the third one said.

More guys piled out of the other pickup trucks to come join their three friends. Within moments I was backed against the chain-link fence. It was like a pack of wolves surrounding a wounded elk.

"Town knows to leave us alone out here," the muscular leader said. He seemed more emboldened now that his posse was around him. "We're not bothering anyone, and no one bothers us."

"As I said, I'm not from around here, and I was just leaving."

I moved to leave, and the leader jumped in my way and poked his finger into my chest. "You'll sit like a good pooch until I say so." The insult garnered laughter from his buddies. "You a cop or something?"

"I'm a nobody," I said, trying not to show emotion.

A couple of the guys laughed, but a quick look from their leader made them stop. I thought of running, but the young kids would outrun me in a heartbeat. My goal to maximize vacation time had incented me to rush through this favor for Luke and led to this stupid first step. Normally, I would have eased my way into a case rather than jump in headfirst and expose myself to a situation like this.

"You gonna cry, old man?"

"Everyone's got a brass pair when a dozen of their friends are with them," I whispered.

"You say something?"

I bit my tongue.

"Speak up, punk!"

Either way, it appeared I was going to get my teeth kicked in, so I made the dumb decision to give them a reason to do it. In my mind, if I was going to get beat up, then I wanted to deserve it. "I said I think you're all a nice bunch of fellas whose mommas must be proud."

The leader took a swing, which I high-forearm blocked. The brief victory gave way to a tidal wave of counterattacks when the pack of guys pounced on me. I managed to give a quick punch to the closest groin I saw but made the tactical decision to just huddle up and take it. I protected my head and kept checking my appendix holster to keep my gun from falling out. A couple of blows hurt, and one or two of them kicked me, but most of the feet landed on my butt and thighs. I kept pawing at my Smith and Wesson wanting to draw it and blast away, but reminded myself these were punk teenagers. Still, every punch hurt, and I didn't know when they would stop or if any of them were carrying weapons or firearms.

"Enough!" someone finally shouted.

The group backed off, keeping their circular formation, while I sat on all fours catching my breath like a panting dog with drool coming from my mouth. I looked around, trying to index faces to memory, but everything was a blur. Nothing in my body seemed broken, so I stood up, holding my side, which was sore. Some of the punks were stoic, but most smiled as if they were proud of themselves. Like they had just accomplished some great feat ganging up on a single man. I glanced over at the girls hanging from the trucks. Some laughed at me, but a few seemed sympathetic. The young brunette girl I was there for was nowhere in sight. The circle opened a space for me, and I exited the gap limping a little, humiliated a lot.

Snickers and jeers from the boys followed as if to tempt me to say something. "Look at him." one said.

"He's scared," another said.

"I bet he's about to cry."

"Probably peed his pants."

"Go home and put your socks and sandals on and head to the beach," another laughed.

A few choice words came to mind, but I remembered the Bible held vast passages about fools and speech. Specifically, Proverbs 18:6 talked about opening your big fat mouth and getting a beatdown for it, which I just did. I ate my proverbial crow and limped away to fight another day.

The moment I rounded the corner of the strip mall and was out of their site, I picked up the pace back to the RV. In the main parking lot, it seemed like another world. A place where moms walked with infants, and SUVs and minivans jockeyed for parking spots. I jumped in the RV, started it up, and tore out of the parking lot just in case the pickup truck gang decided they wanted a go for round two.

Suddenly, a girl's voice spoke from behind me. "That was dumb."

I almost slammed on the brakes before I looked in the rearview mirror. A teenage girl with a short brunette haircut lay on the couch with a book in her hand.

"Marcy?"

She gave me a thumbs-up. "You're the guy staying at my grampy's? I met you last year, and I saw you pull up in this rig the other day."

"Yes, and yes."

"That was very low-key of you back there."

"I just wandered back there and nearly got my teeth kicked in and—"

"Whatever," she said, turning the page of her book.

"It's Brandon."

"Well, Brandon, I know you were looking for me, and I know my grandfather put you up to this."

FOUR

In the rearview mirror, Marcy turned the page of her book, and a moment later, she turned yet another page. Either she was a speed reader, or just had nervous energy and was pretending to read. My face was a little puffy, but there were no bruises or cuts.

"Well, you're right," I said. "I'm here on vacation, but your grandfather did ask me to poke around a bit. He's worried about you."

"I had everything under control until you showed up," she said.

"Whatever you say." I decided to pass by Luke's property and keep driving so we could talk.

"You missed Grampy's farm."

"I know," I said. "Care to tell me what's going on?"

"Not particularly."

"Something to do with your mom?" Marcy didn't respond. I continued onto Mason Avenue. "Are either of you in trouble?"

"None of your business."

I parked the RV. "Whatever. I'm supposed to be on

vacation anyway, and I just got the snot kicked out of me by a bunch of punks on your behalf. I need this about as much as a voluntary root canal."

"That was your choice," she said. "Where we at?"

"I'm sore, I'm mad, and I'm embarrassed," I said. "So I'm doing what any red-blooded male would do in my situation. I'm gonna wash my face, then go get an ice cream." I got up and walked past her to the RV's kitchenette sink and turned on the water pump. After washing my face, I turned to Marcy. "Do I look like I just got beat up by a dozen kids?"

"No. Why?"

"Because my wife will freak out," I said, checking to see if one of my teeth was loose.

She giggled. "You seem more afraid of your wife than that group of guys."

"I fear no man," I said in a mock-heroic tone before lowering my voice. "Only one woman. Come on. Ice cream. My treat."

"Oh, that crap works on seven-year-olds."

"Fine, you can watch me eat my ice cream."

Marcy put the book down with a huff and followed me outside. The nightlife in Cape Charles was bustling with people getting ice cream, leaving the beach, and coming and going from restaurants. We walked up to the window at one of the two ice cream stands downtown, where I ordered a small pistachio.

"This looks good," I said, taking a bite. I didn't say anything else but opened my eyes wide to let Marcy know she was missing out on a delicious dessert.

After a long pause, Marcy said, "Oh, I guess I'll have a black raspberry, please."

Ice cream cones in hand, we started our walk. The night breeze was warm, and a few lights glowed out on the water from fishing boats. The soreness in my lower back, butt, and legs worked itself out after about a hundred yards, and my anger at wanting to throttle those young men who thrashed me also started to dissipate. They were lost souls, I reminded myself.

"So, what do you mean you had everything under control?" I asked.

Marcy licked her ice cream and shrugged her shoulders. "It's a figure of speech."

"I know what a figure of speech is," I said. "It's an idiom."

Marcy slapped her forehead with her free hand. "An idiom is something that has a non-literal meaning attached to a phrase. Like high on the hog. Or he kicked the bucket, or spill the beans—"

"All right," I said. "Gosh, I'm being physically humiliated by young men and intellectually humiliated by a twelve-year-old girl. I quit."

Marcy laughed a little but regained her composure. "I'm sixteen, by the way."

"You into some kind of trouble?"

"Me? No."

"Your mom?" She didn't answer, so I pressed. "Marcy, you strike me as a kid who has their head screwed on straight. So, you were hanging out with a bunch of punks to fit in because of your insecurities?"

"Oh, cut the crap."

"I'm just tweaking you," I said. "Spit it out. You were collecting some sort of data. Doing your own sting operation for some reason?"

"Getting warmer," she said, taking a bite of her cone. "That group of kids sells drugs. It took me months to work my way into their good graces."

"And you were what? Gonna make a citizen's arrest? Give the intel to the cops?"

"Cops won't do anything."

"It's a small town. If those punks are selling drugs, then they must stick out like beacons. There must be cameras on the back side of the grocery store and—"

"There are no cameras on the back of the strip mall," she said. "Besides, they don't sell drugs there, and I think at least one or two of the cops are in on it."

"That's quite a conspiracy," I said.

"Those kids may look stupid, and most of them are, but they're backed by some smart people."

"How so?"

"From what I could gather, the drugs are left at an offsite location, and they're paid in cryptocurrency over wired transactions. Once they get paid, they give the lat-long directions to the buyer. It's genius. No handoffs, no video evidence, nothing. The leader you ran into's name is Jeremy. He's twenty-one and has an IQ around ninety-five, so clearly, some group is backing him with infrastructure and logistics."

"How is this all tied to your mother's job?"

"They get their drugs from a supplier, right?"

"Your mom's job is driving antique cars to dealers, and buyers, all over the eastern seaboard, isn't it?" Marcy didn't respond. "I want to help, but you need to fill in the blanks for me."

Marcy kept silent as a few pedestrians passed by. We meandered down past the massive Cape Charles beach sign that spelled L-O-V-E and onto the public dock. Every ten feet or so, someone had a fishing pole in hand. I peered into a few buckets beside them, but only saw live bait and a few keepers. We stopped at an empty alcove and sat on a wooden built-in bench. I waited for Marcy to speak.

"She's an idiot, you know."

"Who?"

"My mom. But she's the only mom I have." For a moment, I thought Marcy was going to cry, but she seemed to collect herself. "She's involved in something over her head."

"Like?"

"I think she runs drugs in her deliveries."

"And what about the antique cars she delivers?"

"They're just a cover," Marcy said.

"Do you have any proof, or is this a hunch?"

"Sometimes she's broke, and sometimes she's flush with money, but it's always cash. I've never seen her use a credit card unless it's a cash card from the store. And she always has weed."

"That doesn't necessarily mean she's—"

"I haven't finished," Marcy huffed. "Have you seen the cars my mom drives?"

"When I was here last time, I saw one."

"The vehicles are mint condition antiques that get huge dollars at auctions like Barrett-Jackson."

"And?"

"And if they're so valuable, you deliver the cars on a tractor-trailer? It would be one thing if you were selling a single car to a customer a few miles away, but she's driving them a thousand miles to deliver them. You don't put miles like that on an odometer of an antique vehicle. That's idiotic. It devalues them tremendously, not to mention the risk of accidents."

"Yeah, but—"

"No one in the antique car industry does this, Brandon. I've researched it."

I was stumped. Marcy had a good point. "So your mom's personally delivering cars because—"

"Because she's transporting drugs in them. It's a perfect way to go."

"Have you tried to talk to her?"

"Uh, no," Marcy said. "She's too focused on her job and which guy she's dating this month." Marcy pointed across the water to a large stucco building that sat on the water. It looked like an old factory that might have once been a fish processing plant. "That's Cape Charles Customs, where Mom works. "Anything odd stick out to you?"

I stared at the massive, white stucco building. What few windows it had were up high, didn't face the water, and were frosted. "I feel like I'm being tested and failing," I said. "Nothing jumps out at me."

"You are being tested," Marcy said, "and you are failing."

I fought the urge to snap at the cocky teenager. "Okay, relax and let me think for a second. It looks big enough to house a lot of vehicles."

"Go on," she said.

"Windows are high and not facing the water as they'd get blown out during hurricanes."

"Go on."

"Other than that, it looks solid as it should be, as it was built right on the water."

Marcy huffed. "The only thing you got right is it's right on the water. You don't find it odd that a company that restores antique cars works out of an oceanfront piece of real estate that should be a yacht club or a fancy hotel? That property is worth millions. They could repair cars anywhere on the Eastern Shore, but they chose to do it right on the water?"

"That's a valid point, Marcy. However, there are factors you're not considering. Maybe the owners inherited the property from family—"

"No, I've considered everything," Marcy said. "They bought the place through an LLC five years ago. I haven't been able to trace out who the actual owners are. All I know is it's a foreign entity."

"Okay, you've done your homework," I said. "So, what's your conclusion?"

"They're strategically located on the water for a reason."

"And that is for ease of bringing in drugs?" There was an awkward silence. "That's a bit of a stretch."

"You're not talking to some naive teenager, Brandon, so don't insult me. My IQ's one-forty-eight. I don't appreciate your inability to see the obvious. Have you ever heard of Occam's razor?"

"No."

"It's a philosophical problem-solving principle that the simpler path with the fewest assumptions should be chosen."

"And you think your hypothesis does this?"

"Of course. Oh, and by the way, don't think I haven't picked up on your goofiness and joking as an attempt to disarm me. It's a coy, yet manipulative, way to get someone to open up, by the way."

"Okay," I said, holding up my arms in defeat. "And I'll even admit I was being negative up until now, and the evidence you've presented does hold water."

"So you'll help me?"

"I told your grandfather I'd look into your mix-up with that gang. You're clearly not interested in them, so my job's done."

"The job description's been modified," Marcy said. "I need your help to solve this."

"You need my help?" I said. "What are we, Batman and Robin?" She didn't respond. "You're a kid who should be focused on kid stuff, even with your IQ."

"I guess I'll have to keep doing this on my own," Marcy exhaled. "I'll probably be raped and murdered. For what it's worth, enjoy your vacation, and I do appreciate the ice cream." She looked at her cell phone. "It's late. We should probably head back."

After a few deep breaths and a silent prayer, I said, "You are a master manipulator that rivals any woman in my life." I thought I saw a slight smirk appear on her face, but I couldn't tell for sure. Marcy kept her poker face on until I caved in completely. "Okay, I'll look into it, but you gotta promise me you'll stay away from those kids hanging out behind the mall."

"Deal."

"Come on. My wife's gonna be wondering where I am, and don't you have a curfew or something?"

"Not really. Grampy doesn't know what to do with me."

"I don't know what to do with you," I said.

* * *

ON THE DRIVE back to the farm, Marcy sat in the passenger seat. "So, what's the plan?"

"I don't know," I said. "I'm trying to switch my mind from vacation mode to work mode. Let me sleep on it and pray about it. I'll get back to you tomorrow."

"Oh, please tell me you're not one of them."

"One of them?" I said. "You mean a Christian?"

"I follow reason, logic, and science."

"As do I."

Marcy chuckled, "But you think God made the world in a literal seven days? How's that follow science?"

"You think the world, the universe, everything we see around us made itself, which violates reason, logic, and numerous scientific laws?"

"Come on, Brandon. The majority of scientists believe in the big bang."

"That's not a rational response," I said. Marcy's eyes widened as if she were ready for an intellectual boxing match, so I continued. "The majority of scientists believed the world was flat at one point, or that by draining bad blood from someone, you could heal them. So many times throughout history, the majority of scientists were wrong. And not all scientists believe in a big bang the way you do." Marcy was about to speak, but I cut her off. "And the ones you read about are probably in academia, so they have to fall in line, or they'd never get tenure and never get peer-reviewed papers published."

"That's probably the most challenging argument you've presented to me so far," she said.

"You're quite the intellectual snob," I said.

She smiled. "I know."

"It wasn't a compliment," I said. "Oh, and by the way, no Christian I know believes God created everything in seven days."

"Oh really," Marcy said, clearly about to rattle off some statistic.

I parked the RV behind the guesthouse. "It was six days, and He rested on the seventh day."

Marcy shook her head with a combination of a confused and repulsed look. "You're a dork," she said, getting out of the RV. "But you're my only ally right now, so I guess I'm stuck with you."

"Gee, thanks for the compliment, kid. I don't know what I'd do without you." I snapped my fingers. "Oh, yes, I do. I'd enjoy my vacation."

Marcy walked off toward her grandfather's house. Luke greeted her at the door. She kissed him on the cheek before entering. The little atheist had a heart, after all.

Inside the guesthouse, Emily saw the smallest green dot of ice cream on my shirt and announced to the entire house how rude of a Dad I was for getting ice cream without them. So I had to load everyone into the RV and drive them all back into town for their own ice cream cones. Annie tried to ask me where I had been, why my clothes were dirty, and why my face looked puffy, but I changed the subject. She picked up on the cue and knew to wait. It wasn't until we made it to bed later that I could fully explain my story. I left out most of the details of the fight behind the grocery store and just said it was a scuffle.

"You need rest, too, Brandon. We never go on vacation and—"

"I promise I'm just going to poke around a little more. I'm trying to help a nice old man and his granddaughter."

"Okay, but I have a bad feeling this is going to turn into something more than just a favor."

FIVE

The next morning, we hit the beach early. After situating all the toys, chairs, and the umbrella, I walked down to the coffee shop. It was a cloudless sky and already breaking eighty-five. It felt like Southern Florida with the humidity building by the minute. Strange to think that in just a handful of months, I'd be wearing a fleece vest and hat around the farm. I entered the coffee shop and was greeted with the strong scent of freshly ground coffee.

Will was behind the counter, taking orders from a long line of people backed up to the stairwell. "Good morning, Brandon," he said. "I'll be right with you."

"Good morning," I said, standing near the stairwell.

"Hey there," came a familiar Cajun voice from the top of the stairs. I looked up to see an elderly man dressed in a jacket, dress shirt, and bow tie with a worn Bible in front of him.

"Good morning, Mr. Coyne," I said, walking up to greet him. "Looking dapper as usual."

"Care for a seat?"

"I'm just grabbing some coffee before heading back to the beach where my wife and kids are. How's your studying coming?"

"Fascinating," he said. "Moses, Abraham, Joseph, David, Simeon, all had to wait for the right time. Even Jesus waited to reveal himself. Patience is definitely a virtue."

"You waiting on something?"

He shrugged his shoulders and smirked. "If you think of it, we all are."

"Good point," I said.

"How long are you here on vacation?"

"Just a few days."

"I never asked what type of farming you do?"

"I'm a cattle farmer from Nathalie."

He leaned forward and whispered, "And yet you carry a firearm?"

I shrugged. "Living in strange times, Mr. Coyne. Even Jesus said to carry a sword."

"Luke 22:36," he said.

"You do all your studying here, Mr. Coyne?"

"Lately, yes. It's a nice place to focus."

I looked around the empty ornate second-floor room. "I can see what you mean. Well, enjoy the day, sir."

"You as well, son."

* * *

WALKING BACK, I recapped my conversation with Marcy the night before. She had grit for infiltrating this group of kids in an attempt to find out what they were into, but that needed to stop. The girl was highly intelligent. However, was she chasing ghosts, or was she on to something? The part of me that wanted to believe her theories were nothing but tinfoil hat conspiracies was the lazy part that wanted to enjoy the vacation. I had somehow convinced myself that by working multiple jobs and long days on the farm, I deserved this time off. The reality was that this thing called *a vacation* was a first-world blessing that only came about in the past hundred and fifty years or so. Prior to that, it never existed, except for the few elite. The truth was that millions of my brothers and sisters in Christ still lived in either slave-like conditions or were considered subhuman in places like North Korea, China, and parts of the Middle East. I was spoiled to even get a few days off a year.

Golf carts drove along the street as if to tempt me back into vacation mode rather than work. There was something peaceful about seeing an elderly man drive by in a battery-powered golf cart in a Hawaiian print shirt. As if to squash that thought, the next vehicle to pass by was a truck I'd recognize anywhere. It was a new white pickup truck that had been modified to be a lowrider. It had to be the same one that followed me back in Halifax. There couldn't be two trucks like this on the entire east coast. What was it doing here? The truck continued past me and turned onto Pine Street. I couldn't see who was driving, but the license plate confirmed it was the same vehicle. My time in Cape Charles was getting stranger by the minute. I'd have to back burner that coincidence for now.

I made it back to the RV, proud of myself for only eating one muffin. Inside the vehicle, I changed into my bathing suit. At the beach, everyone was on the blanket, but it looked like no one was having fun.

"I have breakfast," I said. "Who wants muffins, and who wants croissants?"

"Dad," Emily said. "You're never going to believe this—"

"There was another shark attack," Amber finished the statement.

"Where?" I said, turning to Annie, who held the small radio up to her ear.

"They've just announced it. It was up the coast a bit. Off of Eastville. The victim was a fifteen-year-old boy."

"How bad?"

"Might lose his leg," she said, turning up the radio.

The news announcer was in the middle of the story. "The National Oceanic and Atmospheric Administration are sending a team down from Woods Hole, Massachusetts. There has never been a recorded shark attack in the Chesapeake Bay. They believe both attacks are due to climate change. Stay tuned for more reports throughout the day."

I looked out over the calm bay water. There were a few swimmers in the water. No one other than our family seemed to know what was going on. I looked up the location of Eastville on my cell phone and realized it was only a few towns over. This second shark attack was closer. It didn't make sense. The bay water was brackish as it was where the Chesapeake flowed into the ocean, so not many sharks would enjoy swimming in the lower salt content water. Then again, bull sharks were known for being able to survive in freshwater and did attack people nearly as much as great whites or tiger sharks.

"Brandon?"

"Huh?"

"I asked if you think it's okay for the kids to go in the water?"

"Sure," I said. These are freak accidents. "Besides, the chances of getting bitten are—"

"A million to one," Amber finished my sentence. "Tell that to the two people who got chomped, Brandon."

"Come on," I said. "We've waited months for this vacation, and I'm not gonna let a few shark attacks stop us." I took off my shirt and headed toward the water.

"That's not funny, Daddy," Emily said, catching up with me.

I dove into the warm water and swam out a bit before wading back toward the shallows where Amber and Emily waited. I didn't tell them, but I disliked the fact the bay water was murky, and visibility was not very good. Sharks had bad eyesight, and the poor visibility may have contributed to the attacks. The animals might have mistaken humans for some other prey in their regular diet.

Emily's eyes widened, and she pointed behind me. "Daddy!"

I swung around, expecting to see a fin cutting through the water toward us. About fifty yards away, a couple of fins did, in fact, cut through the water. They were parallel to shore and submerged a moment later. Peace immediately took the place of panic.

"It's okay. Come here, sweetie," I said. Emily waded out to meet me. I picked her up. "That's a pod of dolphins. If there are dolphins nearby, then it's probably safe to swim."

"Are you sure?"

"I'm sure," I said. "They're natural enemies of sharks."

* * *

Eventually, everyone made their way to the water, including Annie and the baby. Everyone stayed in the shallows, though. We left for lunch and returned for the afternoon. By this time, news seemed to have gotten out about the second shark attack, and only a few people were in the water. On the beach, Emily and Amber both read from different *Nancy Drew* books. Amber seemed to be vicariously reliving her childhood through her young stepsister. It was sweet to watch how well they got along. Emily looked up to Amber as a highly intelligent older sister who she could talk to about everything from makeup to math. Yet, at times, I'd find Emily explaining certain passages of the Bible to Amber as she was a new believer.

* * *

MIDAFTERNOON, I brought Addison into the RV to let her nap. I lowered the coffee table to make it into a bed and sat across from her on the couch. She was a clone of Annie and Emily, with dark hair, brown eyes, and pale skin. She lay with a thin blanket and worn teddy bear under her arm and quickly fell asleep. I used the opportunity to lay across from her on the RV's couch and quietly thanked God for my family and the ability to go on vacation.

Like so many times before, my mind naturally drifted to my son, Jonah. My heart ached for the boy we lost in a car accident years prior. He would have loved this vacation and the beach, and he would have adored his baby sister. The memory, that never became reality, snuck out of my eye and rolled down my cheek.

I awoke an hour later to the sound of the back door to the RV opening. It was Emily coming in to use the bathroom. She gave a thumbs-up to let me know everything was okay. I found a beach towel and rolled over, using the towel as a makeshift blanket. I was starting to relax a little, but I did have work to do.

* * *

AFTER THE BEACH, we all showered and dressed up to go into town for dinner. There was a nice waterfront restaurant set in a gated community in Cape Charles. We were seated outside on a deck and watched as patrons came up to the restaurant by fancy boats, kayaks, and even stand-up paddleboards. The sun hadn't set yet, and the breeze brought with it clean salt air that seemed to cleanse your lungs. I ordered crabs covered in Old Bay Seasoning. Annie and Amber each ordered a salad with grilled chicken, and Emily opted for a wood-fired grilled cheese on homemade bread.

We fed Addison a little from each of our meals. She loved the crab most and kept wanting more. After dinner was ice cream, followed by a walk along the pier. I excused myself back to the RV to use the bathroom. In my go bag was my emergency gear which held a first aid kit and other gadgets I used for work. Zip handcuffs, spare magazines for my nine-millimeter, a backup flashlight, glow sticks, as well as a fixed blade knife. From a side pouch, I grabbed a monocular and walked down Mason Avenue. I crossed over into the parking lot behind the Veterans War Memorial. Across an expanse of water was the massive stucco facility that was Cape Charles Customs.

Through the monocular, I zoomed in to see a car hauler outside the facility loaded with an early '70s Camaro and a late '60s Ford Mustang. They were the only two vehicles on a rig that could hold nine cars. From what

I could see, neither of the vehicles seemed to need any work, but I wasn't an antique car expert. The vehicles could be there for interior upholstery or engine work. There was no activity around the facility. Beyond the building was a Coast Guard station. Would a drug syndicate, using a car restoration business as a front, really park itself next to a branch of the US military? Utter stupidity or absolute genius, I couldn't decide. Marcy had a point, though. Why would Cape Charles Customs utilize an expensive waterfront facility when they could repair cars a few miles away from a cheap prefab metal barn?

An arm wrapped around my waist, followed by the floral smell of Annie's organic shampoo. "Whatcha doing, handsome?"

"Scoping out that facility," I said, pointing across the water. "Luke's daughter-in-law works there. There's a slight chance it may not be simply an antique automobile restoration business."

"Such as?"

"Drug running," I whispered.

Annie took the monocular and peered across the water. "You have doubts about that theory?"

"I don't know. There's definitely cause for looking into it based on what I've learned. On the other hand, it just seems too far-fetched when I say it out loud."

Annie handed the monocular back. "Then why's there someone on the roof walking back and forth like they're on patrol? Looks like security on top of some embassy in a foreign land?"

I took the monocular and looked. Sure enough, a mid-twenties white male was on the roof, dressed in black 5.11 pants and a loose-fitting black shirt, who hadn't been there moments earlier. There was a bulge under his right side, which told me he had a sidearm under the shirt. He held binoculars in his hands. I shifted my view from the roof toward the water to look for anything he might be waiting to see. Nothing stuck out to me. A moment later, Amber came up pushing Addison's carriage, followed by Emily.

"Whatcha looking at?" Emily asked.

"Just taking in the beautiful view of the landscape around us," I said. "Then again, your momma's standing right next to me."

"That's so cheesy."

Amber squinted her eyes. She clearly knew something was up but didn't say anything.

* * *

BACK AT THE GUESTHOUSE, Annie and I sat outside and watched a handful of stars come out. Emily put Addison down to bed in the pack 'n play, while Amber made some phone calls in her bedroom. The breeze was warm, and there were no mosquitos. I leaned back in the Adirondack chair and exhaled.

"You relaxed?" Annie asked.

"I'm trying."

"But you keep thinking about Luke and his family?" I didn't respond. "Can't you tell them you're on vacation?"

"Imagine if God said that to us when we were in need? He'd be like, hey Brandon, I heard ya prayer about your kid being sick, but I'm on vacation right now. I'll circle back with you soon."

"I know," Annie exhaled, "but I feel bad for you. You never get a break. You work on the farm nonstop, then run off to these crazy side jobs and—"

"Sweetie, I love being a cattle farmer. It's just not

enough to make ends meet. And honestly, I don't mind most of the side PI work."

"Well, I do. Since you met Roger Drake and Senator Schilling, your work seemed to jump from small-town insurance fraud cases to life-or-death scenarios overnight."

I reached for her hand and spoke a rhetorical question I'd mentioned a hundred times before. "Who's in control?"

"I know," she said, pointing to the sky. "I just selfishly want you to turn this one job down and enjoy the beach with us."

A scooter pulled onto the farm's gravel driveway, spraying up dust. The driver had on goggles, a bicycle helmet, and a purple backpack. It was Marcy. She veered off the main trunk of the driveway, pulled up to us, and shut down the scooter.

"How many cc's that bad boy have?" I asked, pointing to her scooter.

"Fifty," she said, patting the engine like it was a massive Harley Davidson. "She's got it where it counts, though."

"Marcy, this is my wife, Annie."

Annie got up and walked over to shake her hand. "Nice to meet you."

"Wow, Brandon, you married up."

Annie laughed. "I like this girl."

Marcy came over with her book bag. "Thought any more about what we talked about?"

"I did."

"And, you got a plan yet?"

"I'm going to poke around some more. Just make sure you stay away from those kids behind the grocery store."

"No problem. I was about to cut my losses anyway,"

she said. "Took me a long time to work my way into their group. Had to try smoking weed and drink a couple of beers to do it, which I hated."

"Oh my gosh," Annie said.

"Then I had to learn about their drug system, all the while fending off sexual advances from, like, three different boys."

"You're stressing me out," Annie said. "I don't even know you, but I'd be paranoid if you were my daughter."

"Don't worry, Mrs. Hall, I carry pepper spray."

"You're a beautiful, young girl," Annie said. "Please be careful. Brandon, why aren't you helping this girl?"

I turned to Annie, my mouth open as if to say, *That's completely opposite of what you said a minute ago.*

Marcy plopped her backpack on a wooden table next to me. "So, what's the plan, Brandon?"

"I'll leave you two alone," Annie said. "I'm going inside to make sure the baby went down. Nice to meet you, Marcy."

"You too, Mrs. Hall."

After Annie left, I asked, "How come she gets the Mrs. Hall treatment, and I just get Brandon?"

"I like her," Marcy said, straight-faced.

"You're a funny kid."

Marcy sat down in Annie's Adirondack chair and opened her backpack. She took out a cute notebook decorated with butterflies and proceeded to sharpen a number two pencil with an old Buck pocketknife I assumed might have been her dad's. I peered inside the backpack and was greeted with a book on maritime law, one on the history of Cape Charles, and another thin book on the history of the Cape Charles Coast Guard Station.

"Research," she said, acknowledging my snooping. "Now I've been thinking—"

"I'm sure you have."

She ignored my snide remark. "The kids I hung around with behind the strip mall are definitely connected to whatever my mom's company is doing. I'm ninety-nine percent sure it's drugs, but I'm not ruling out other things like guns."

"What makes you so sure of all of this?"

I've seen them make some deals while I was there. Like I said, nothing was passed. It was all done over phones. The head kid you tussled with, Jeremy, he handles everything. He's paid in crypto, and from what I can gather, would send the buyers directions where the product, or the drugs, were located for pickup. It was a two-tier system."

"What do you mean?"

"They would pay a deposit in crypto, and he'd give them directions. Once they get to the location, they'd find the drugs, or product, locked somehow. They'd pay Jeremy a second payment of crypto over an app, and then he'd send them a combination to the lock, or locker, via some other secure messenger system that self-deletes."

"Pretty ingenious if true," I said.

"It's true."

"Where's Mom fit in?"

Marcy held up her hand. "You're getting ahead of yourself."

I tried not to chuckle at the rebuke from the sixteen-year-old. "My apologies. Please proceed, professor."

"Jeremy and all his guys are too stupid to set up a system this complex. Heck, half of them can't even set up their email. The only reason I figured this out was I uploaded a virus to Jeremy's cell phone via a networked game they all play. Then, when they panicked when their phones crashed, there I was like a miracle worker who knew how to fix all their phones."

"And you used the opportunity to download some of their data." Marcy gave me a thumbs-up. "Find anything that tied them to Cape Charles Customs?"

She shook her head. "No, whatever messenger system they use is encrypted, but I did find a couple of emails between a Sergeant Cox to Jeremy using Proton Mail talking about picking up a car at Cape Charles Customs."

"That doesn't mean—"

"Brandon, a cop emailing a teen drug dealer using a secure email chain mentioning Cape Charles Customs in the same sentence?"

"Okay. So let's assume it's drugs for the time being," I said. "And let's assume your friend's entire setup was done by an outside source. And, for the time being, let's assume Cape Charles Customs was tied in, or that actual source."

"Brandon, don't talk down to me. We're well beyond assumptions. I'm not like you with blind faith. I already told you I researched the history of Cape Charles Customs LLC, and the owner is somewhere in South America. They have been in business for years, and there's only, like, a handful of people who work there." Before I could ask, Marcy said, "I've watched them for months and counted only four male employees and two females, not including my mom. Only a couple of antique cars come through there each month, and the vehicles are always in mint condition. There's no way they could stay in business with that few products flowing through their doors while maintaining a facility that massive. Also, no antique car restoration company delivers antique cars by driving them a thousand miles. They're always trailered." I didn't say anything for a good thirty seconds. Marcy cleared her throat. "You know I'm right."

"And the cops are what? All paid off?"

"I have reason to believe at least a few have been paid off, but it's impossible to say who's legit and who's not."

"And the Coast Guard?"

"They're literally next door," Marcy said. "I can't believe some of them aren't involved. I admit, that part is all speculation at this point."

"Have you tried to reach anyone at the federal level?"

"I don't know anyone in the DEA, and don't trust anyone in the FBI after what I've seen them pull lately. All the alphabet agencies seem suspicious with their behavior over the past few years. Targeting political opposition, false flags, etc. It all gives me the creeps."

I chuckled. "I tend to agree. So, your mom's just a driver who's been sucked into all this?" Marcy nodded. "And your goal is to what? Gather enough evidence so you can go to someone honest in government and—"

"Broker a deal for her amnesty," Marcy said. "If I can find someone I trust in government."

I sat back in the chair, stewing on what she said. "Where's your mom now?"

"She's two days late," Marcy exhaled, "but that's not unusual."

"Does your mom know that you suspect anything?"

Marcy shook her head back and forth. Her dark hair reminded me of an older version of Emily. Unlike Emily, Marcy had short hair, darker skin, and blue eyes. "That's what I got," she said. "We need a plan?"

"I'm still not sure," I said. "I can't wrap my head around this entire thing yet."

"Believe me. It's real."

"Gonna think and pray on it some more."

"Ugh. You and my grandfather are cut from the same cloth."

"And you're an enlightened freethinker molded by her secular education who thinks she's above all this?" I leaned in. "Let me tell you a little secret, kiddo. You may be smart, even a genius, but smarter people than you throughout history have thrown everything they can at the Bible and have come away from it either frustrated to no end or believing in Jesus."

"I'll believe when I have empirical proof."

"The entire Bible is a paradox. The first shall be last. You are strong when you are weak. If you want to be the greatest, then you must be a servant. The irony is that many times the Bible reveals itself with empirical proof after you come to faith. Once you believe, only then do you start to see mathematical miracles and answers to prayers that could only come from God. Jesus said it in the Sermon on the Mount in Matthew. Seek ye first the kingdom of Heaven."

"Whatever you say, but sounds like a Ponzi scheme to me."

"You're all of sixteen, and intelligence without wisdom and experience can be dangerous. You're a very smart girl, Marcy, but you lack humility."

"Give me a break," she spat, picking up her backpack. "I lost my dad when I was a kid and now have to worry about my mother like she's some knucklehead teenager. I think I've lived enough life experience to know up from down and right from wrong. Sorry if I don't genuflect when you say, Jesus. You know what, enjoy your vacation."

She jumped on her scooter and started it up. My

immediate impulse was to chase after her, wag my finger in her face, and continue to argue. Tell her she was acting like a brat. That I was the one doing her a favor by giving up my vacation. That she wasn't the only one who's dealt with loss. She had no idea the loss my family had been through, and the loss I'd seen friends and family endure. Before I could say anything further, Marcy sped off toward Luke's house.

I searched my memory for any biblical passage that allowed me to tell a nonbelieving teen to suck it up when they were upset, but I couldn't think of one. After a few deep breaths and a quick prayer, I was convicted. My apologetic pitch was fine, but my follow-through insult was poor form. I was wrong and had stepped over the line. What Marcy had experienced before she turned sixteen was traumatic, and what she was dealing with regarding her mom was an unfair burden to put on any young girl, especially one without a spiritual compass. I was commanded to rejoice with those who rejoiced and to weep with those who weep. I started to walk toward Luke's house to apologize but saw that all the lights were off. My apology would have to wait until morning.

SIX

I DIDN'T SLEEP WELL THAT NIGHT, KNOWING THIS YOUNG girl was probably stewing over our argument. I had to apologize to her and make things right. The next morning, I was up before everyone else and found Luke out in the barn working on a small Evinrude outboard motor.

"That a two- or four-stroke engine?"

"Huh? Oh, good morning, Brandon. It's a two-stroke." He pointed to the back of the barn where an old Starcraft wooden boat sat on a trailer. "I want to get back out on the water to take Marcy fishing."

"Is Marcy around?"

"She usually sleeps in. Why?"

I filled Luke in on our discussions and Marcy's conclusions about her mom's job and its real responsibilities.

"It kind of makes sense to me now," he said, placing a wrench down. "Cassie's job, her descent into a mess. Everything."

"So, you think Marcy's right about Cassie's job being a front?"

"Brandon, my granddaughter's not one for melodrama, never was. She always walked around with her face in a book. Heck, when her mom would punish her, it would never be the threat of no television or video games. It always involved taking her books away. I'm telling you, she's right."

"Okay, I believe you," I said. "I'm gonna go check out Cape Charles Customs today."

"Do you want company?"

I waved him off. "I'd rather just go myself after I drop everyone off at the beach."

"Keep me posted, and thank you for everything."

"Don't thank me. I haven't done anything yet. When Marcy wakes up, please call me. I need to talk to her."

* * *

ONCE THE FAMILY was in the RV, we repeated our morning tradition of stopping at the coffee shop. I went in to order iced coffees for me and Annie, tea for Amber, and a smoothie for Emily, along with croissants. With the order in hand, I walked upstairs to see if my friend was there. Charles Coyne was at his normal table facing his Bible and notebook. A new table had been set up for what looked like an upcoming function.

"How's the studying going?"

"Great," he said. There was a long, awkward pause. Charles spoke without looking up from whatever he was writing. "I sense you have a question."

"How long have you lived here?"

"Moved here about twelve years ago," he said, stopping his writing to stare at the fancy tin ceiling. "No, that was ten years ago."

"You still practice law?"

"No. I'm strictly retired and do some academic advising at a Christian college or two."

"You familiar with businesses around here?"

"I'm aware of what goes on if that's what you mean?"

I bit my lip. I needed to pick my words carefully. I didn't have the luxury of knowing the layout and way things worked in Cape Charles, but I also didn't have the luxury of time to find out. "You ever see anything out of the ordinary?"

Charles placed his pen down and looked at me with a kind smile. "Mr. Hall, it's a beach town during summer. The two attract weird like a politician to a fundraiser. You need to be more specific."

"What do you know of the businesses around Mason Avenue and downtown Cape Charles?" Charles raised his eyebrows as if to say that I was being way too vague. "You ever hear of any abnormal activity?"

He gave a slight smile. "I thought you were a cattle farmer?"

"I do a little PI work on the side."

"And I take it your vacation was hijacked by some of this side work?"

"You don't miss a thing, do you?"

Charles closed his Bible but continued to write in his notebook as if he were finishing a thought. "Cape Charles is pretty calm. There's not a lot of criminal activity here. We're below the national average in most metrics."

"Who said anything about criminal activity?"

"I'm assuming your PI work revolves around more than just cattle trampling neighbors' fences. Besides, what else could drag you off a gorgeous vacation unless it was something like crime."

"Well, now that you mention it, Charles. You ever hear of any criminal activity going on around town?"

He finished writing and closed his journal. "Not really. It's usually pretty calm here. Unless, of course, you count Cape Charles Customs."

My jaw fell open, and I nearly dropped the food and drink order.

"I take it that's what your case involves?" I didn't respond. Charles started to place his work into a worn leather briefcase. "Why don't we go for a walk, Brandon."

* * *

A MINUTE LATER, we exited the coffee shop. Outside at the RV, I introduced the rest of the family to Charles. I handed out the breakfast and told Annie that Charles and I were going to walk down to the beach.

"Good morning, Mr. Coyne," Emily said from the backseat of the RV.

Charles did a mock bow again. "Nice to see you again, Emily."

"Can I walk with you guys?" Emily asked.

"Next time, sweetie. I need to pick Mr. Coyne's brain for a minute. I'll see you at the beach."

After Annie drove off, Charles led me down Mason Avenue. He adjusted his bow tie and fixed the leather shoulder strap on his briefcase. I walked and sipped my iced coffee like a little kid waiting for a circus performer to show me another trick.

Finally, I couldn't take it any longer. "Charles, how?" He didn't respond, and we kept walking in silence, and finally, I burst out. "You're killing me here. Where are you pulling that info from on Cape Charles Customs?"

"It's not a secret what they do," he said. "It's just that no one has had the spine to do anything about it."

"Seriously?"

"Capone had the entire city of Chicago paid off," he said. "Why couldn't a few cogs in the wheels of a small town like Cape Charles be greased?"

"But it's the twenty-first century. Surely with cell phones and satellites, this would get out?" Charles didn't respond. "Seriously?"

"Human nature doesn't change."

"What's their deal?"

Charles waited for an elderly couple to pass us by before talking further. "Cape Charles Customs is connected to MS-13 in South America and is one of their proxies who run drugs stateside. Once, years ago, the Feds raided the place but found nothing. Since then, local PD seems to stay away, and Coast Guard is busy doing Coast Guard things. People around here are busy with life and enjoying themselves and are, as the Bible says, willingly ignorant to things."

"But you're convinced they're still running drugs?"

"I am."

"So is a friend of mine."

"So, what are you going to do about it?"

"Me?"

"God is faithful."

"Huh?"

"Why do you think I've been studying passages on patience? I had been praying God would send someone to fix Cape Charles's drug problem. It seems law enforcement won't touch it, and after a lot of prayers, here you are."

"Charles, the type of PI work I do usually involves little things like insurance fraud cases. We're talking MS-

13 here. The gang has more money and infrastructure than some countries."

"And David was a shepherd who slew a giant with a piece of leather and a stone," Charles said. Before I could reply, he hit me with a passage from First Corinthians. "And God has chosen the weak things of the world to shame the things which are strong."

"I admit I'm weak, but I think you got the wrong guy, Charles."

He shrugged his shoulders. "Maybe." He stopped and turned to me with ice-blue eyes that seemed to look through me. "Be not forgetful to entertain strangers: for thereby some have entertained angels unawares."

"Hebrews 13:2," I said.

"I wondered since the first day we met whether you were a stranger or an angel?"

I chuckled. "Charles, I'm the furthest thing from an angel."

He bit his lip as if he didn't believe me. "Well, this is where I turn off. Be safe, and while you're down at the beach, make sure to walk the sandy shore to fill your sling with stones."

* * *

AT THE BEACH, Amber and Emily had the baby in knee-deep water while Annie sat in her beach chair watching from beneath her sun hat and sunglasses. She still looked like the young woman I married years ago. She didn't seem to age even after giving birth to three children.

I walked up and kissed her. "Did you finish your book?"

"No. I just can't focus when the kids are in the water. I keep looking for a shark's fin to pop up."

"I think those were two freak accidents," I said.

"There's never been shark attacks in the Chesapeake Bay before. And there's been two in a week. The math doesn't add up. NOAA thinks it's climate change."

"I doubt it," I said. "Maybe overfishing has caused apex predators to move in? Then again, overregulation has stifled the fishing industry, so the fish populations may have grown. This could have brought the sharks closer to shore to feed." I thought for a moment. "It could also be similar to the case of the 1916 New Jersey shark attacks that the book *Jaws* was based upon."

"What was that?"

I waved my hand back and forth like I didn't believe the scenario of what I was about to say. "Forget it."

"Spit it out, Brandon."

"There were a string of attacks in New Jersey in a span of twelve days that many believe was the result of a single rogue shark killing several people."

"Why would a shark do that?"

I winced. "Some believe the animal was a freak of nature who got a taste for humans and liked it."

Annie got up and went out to the shallows to remove Addison from Emily's arms. On her way back to the chair, she shouted over her shoulder. "Stay in shallow water, girls."

FOR LUNCH, we walked down Mason Avenue to a sub shop. After lunch, the girls went shopping while I wandered a few blocks over to Cape Charles Customs. I wore a baseball cap and sunglasses to help hide my face as I assumed there were security cameras onsite. The parking lot was surrounded by a chain-link fence topped with barbed wire. The entrance had an automatic gate that had been left open. I took this as an invitation to let myself onto the property. A fancy new diesel pickup sat outside the massive stucco building next to the antique Camaro and Mustang I had seen previously on the car hauler. I noted that both antique cars could handle the speeds on modern highways. There were no Model T Fords here. The diesel truck had a rebel flag sticker on the rear glass along with a local dive shop sticker.

"Can I help you?" came a voice from somewhere off to my right. I turned to see a tall, muscular man with a perfectly manicured beard, mirrored sunglasses, a tight-fitting button-down shirt, a massive belt buckle, skinny jeans, and what looked like alligator, or ostrich, cowboy boots.

"You the owner?"

"Maybe," he said.

I gave my best aw-shucks smile. "I'm thinking of getting my '68 Mustang Fastback fixed up so I can sell it at an auction. I heard you guys were good."

"Who referred you?"

I panicked and had to think quick. "Guy I met at the local coffee shop."

"We're backed up a few months, and I only work on referrals."

I pointed to the two antique muscle cars. "You don't look that backed up."

"We have a load of vehicles coming in any day that we need to work on, but like I said, I only work on referrals. Who'd you say referred you?"

I ignored the question and walked up to the Camaro. "This beauty looks like she doesn't need a thing. You guys do engine, body, and upholstery because I mostly need bodywork—"

The man's cell phone rescued me from the awkward situation.

He answered the phone with a quick "Yeah?"

His eyes followed me as I walked around the cars. When I turned back, he was still watching me while he spoke on the phone. I gave him a thank-you wave, pulled out my phone, and pretended to take a call. He clearly suspected I was a Fed or something. Cape Charles Customs had no real inventory, and if the business was legit, they'd be begging for customers. I had never heard of an auto body, or any business like this, working on referrals only. I wandered out of the property and met the girls back at the RV. Annie and Emily were sunburned and wanted to head back to shower and hang out at the guesthouse before dinner.

* * *

AT THE HOUSE, I showered first so I could start dinner. The guesthouse came with a propane grill, which I fired up for a steak dinner. Overhead, Luke flew in his biplane, the waning red sun acted like a perfect backdrop for the antique plane. He didn't seem to be dusting crops or doing anything other than enjoying himself.

While the grill warmed, Marcy entered the property on her scooter. She drove past me, parked at Luke's house, and went inside. A few minutes later, she got back on the scooter and drove over to the guesthouse. She pulled up just as I placed the last steak on the grill.

"Just in time for dinner," I said. "You bring an appetite?"

"You still mad?"

"I'm not mad, and I want to apologize for upsetting you last night. I was out of line."

"I'm sorry for storming off as well," she said, putting the scooter up on a kickstand. Marcy plopped down in an Adirondack chair. She looked into the cooler next to the grill and took out a bottle of water. She took a sip and then pressed the cold bottle against her forehead.

"Help yourself," I joked.

She ignored the comment. "Mom did it again."

"What did she do?"

"Found out why she was late. She got in an accident."

"Is she okay?"

"Sprained her wrist, I think," Marcy huffed.

"You don't seem too concerned?"

"Oh, she'll be fine. She's going to some MinuteClinic to get her wrist X-rayed, but she's more stressed about the car."

"I'm sorry," I said. "Anything I can do?"

"Can you snap your fingers and fix everything?"

"Wish I could, Marcy. In fact, we're only supposed to be here a couple more days. I'm not sure what I can accomplish—"

"I need you to do something with the time you do have, Brandon."

I lifted the grill lid. All of the steaks were too rare. "You sure you're only sixteen and not, like, seventy?"

"Mom is the child, and I'm the adult. It's the way it is, and I just have to accept it. 'Bout as dysfunctional as it gets."

For a moment, it looked like Marcy might start to cry. She winced as if forcing her emotions back down inside. I felt bad for her. She was robbed of a childhood and had no spiritual support system. I prayed as to what I could say that might offer some comfort.

Marcy exhaled. "Why couldn't I have a normal family

like yours? Why'd I get stuck with a loser for a mother and—"

A moment later, she dropped her head in her hands and did start to cry. Annie was far better at consoling than I was, but she was nowhere in sight.

I dropped down on a knee and rested a hand on Marcy's shoulder. "Can I just say a simple prayer, please?"

Marcy wiped her eyes. "Whatever, Brandon."

"Lord, please be with my friend, Marcy. She needs to know you and know our Father in Heaven will never leave nor forsake her. I pray this in Jesus's name."

"Thanks," she said.

Suddenly, Emily's voice broke the silence from inside the house. "Mommy, Addison got into your pocketbook and wrote all over herself with your lipstick!"

I winced. Even from outside, I could hear the combination of exhale and huff from Annie. "Addison, you naughty girl! Brandon, this is your daughter!"

Amber's voice joined the pack. "Can everyone stop yelling? I'm on the phone."

I giggled, and Marcy burst out laughing.

"Welcome to our normal family," I said.

Marcy wiped her eyes and took the spatula from me. "Go check on your family. I got this."

* * *

WE ATE DINNER OUTSIDE. Luke came over and joined us with a batch of fresh corn on the cob. It was a last-minute picnic that turned out to be a nice gathering. Marcy seemed to get along well with Emily and Amber. She connected with Amber on an intellectual level. They went back and forth, finishing each other's sentences. I knew Amber was sharp but didn't realize how smart until Marcy and her started playing some brainiac trivia game on Amber's cell phone after dinner. I was embarrassed I couldn't answer half the science and math questions they did. Later that night in bed, I confessed to Annie that I didn't know what I could do with the time remaining.

"Did you pray about it?"

"Yeah, and I feel like I should do something, but—"

"Then do something."

"Like?"

"Anything," she said. "Just take a few steps and see what doors open."

"And what about our timetable and—"

"Let God work out the details."

"But—"

"Trust in the Lord with all thine heart; and lean not unto thine own understanding."

"Just start moving in a direction and let Him guide your steps."

SEVEN

The next morning, Amber and Emily made everyone pancakes. After breakfast, I dropped the girls at the beach. Although crowded, it had fewer people in the water than the day before. What few dared to wade in stayed around the shallows. A hundred yards offshore, a small Boston Whaler Coast Guard boat patrolled back and forth. I zoomed in with my cell phone's camera and could see there was a bolt-action rifle attached to the center console. They were patrolling for sharks.

Annie would only let Addison in the water if she was with her. I forced myself to repeat the statistics about shark attacks and the low probability of any more happening. Still, I didn't want to leave them, but I had to try a couple of things before we left Cape Charles. If, for no other reason than to clear my conscience. In less than ten minutes of searching on my smartphone, I was able to pull up the address of the cop named Cox who lived in Cape Charles. It took less than five minutes on Google Earth for me to see a rough picture of the home, which was located on the bay.

"Annie, mind if I go rent a kayak for a bit?"

"Are you sure it's safe?"

"You mean in case of sharks?" She nodded. "The boats are like fifteen feet long. Besides, I'm just gonna paddle around the shoreline. I want to chase down a lead."

"Okay, but be careful."

I went back to the RV and got the monocular from my bag, along with a bottle of water and a PowerBar. My cell phone case was waterproof, but I still put it in a floating ziplock beach baggy. I walked down the beach and found the teenage boy vendor sitting under an umbrella playing on his cell phone. I paid him for a two-hour rental. After a quick mandatory instruction and life vest fitting, I was off. I had kayaked plenty of times before, so it was easygoing. When I paddled by the girls on shore, Emily stood up, hands on hips, shouting something I couldn't quite make out. I assumed she was mad I had left her behind.

I paddled a bit closer. "I'm just getting in a quick workout. Be back in a bit."

"You're rude," she said. "You didn't even ask if I wanted to come."

"Next time, sweetie. Look after your little sister."

"Watch out for fins in the water," Amber said.

"I'll be fine," I said.

As if on cue, a ton of bait fish jumped out of the water all around me, pursued by something beneath them. I paddled hard to get out of the area just in case the predator chasing the fish was something bigger than striped bass. Beyond the beach was a small inlet where a man fly fished from the reeds with a puppy sitting next to him. I continued paddling north, periodically looking down at my cell phone for directions. The cop's house was another half mile down the shore. In the distance, a dolphin broke the surface. It coincided with the sun reflecting off the water. It was a spectacular site, with the breeze a perfect remedy to offset the blistering sun. Fifteen minutes later, I floated a couple of hundred yards off the back side of the house, or mansion. It was the gaudiest thing I had ever seen. It was mostly glass facing the water. From what I could see, the sides were white stucco. It looked like someone gave a seven-year-old a blank check and said, put on a blindfold and go design a house. I laid the paddle in the kayak bracket and lifted the monocular from around my neck. The backyard was average, maybe a quarter of an acre with a small plunge pool. There was an early fifties female sunbathing topless in a lounge chair by the pool. Her skin was a dark leathery brown color. The kind that looked like it had been overexposed in the sun for decades. Next to her was a half-empty bottle of champagne in a bucket.

"Little early to be boozing, lady," I said.

Surrounding her in the yard were a dozen landscapers, seemingly oblivious to the half-naked lady sunbathing a few yards from them. After a few moments, an overweight, bald, mid-forties male in a police uniform exited the back door of the home and walked up to the female. Words were exchanged. The sunbathing female used her hand to cover her eyes but didn't bother to cover her chest. A moment later, she threw a champagne glass at the man. It shattered on some hard piece of equipment on his police utility belt. He shook his head, did an about-face, and exited the way he came.

"A McMansion on the water is a stupid way to flaunt your crooked money," I whispered to no one in particular.

The sound of a boat horn from somewhere behind

snapped me from my spying mode. I dropped the monocular and casually picked up the paddle.

"Hey, you!"

I turned around to act as oblivious as possible. The Coast Guard Boston Whaler floated fifteen yards away. Two young twenty-something muscle-bound guys were on board and did not look happy. A darker-haired one with a mustache shouted something, but I acted like I couldn't hear him over the rumble of the dual engine.

"What's your problem, guy?"

"Oh, I'm just paddling around," I said.

"Why the interest in this house?"

Out of the corner of my eye, I could see the landscapers starting to watch from the property. The last thing I needed was my picture taken or my name flagged on a list that could make its way back to MS-13.

"You got any ID on you?" The first sailor said.

"Sorry, I don't, but I gotta fess up, fellas," I said. "A naked lady is sunbathing over there in the yard."

"Shut up!" Immediately the mustached sailor lifted a pair of massive binoculars. "Dang, he's right, Billy. Take a look."

As he handed off the glasses, I started to paddle off. "Caught me red-handed."

As I paddled away, I heard one of them say, "That's Cox's lady."

"She was a trophy wife at one point. Sure let herself go."

"You boys have a good one," I said.

"Stay out of this area, guy," the mustached sailor said, reaching for the binoculars. "It's a heavy traffic lane."

"Will do."

Paddling back, it was obvious these two guys knew the cop and his wife by name. Cape Charles was a small town, and it was not unusual for people to know one another. However, military people were transient and, a lot of times, stayed separate from communities. Back at the beach, Annie asked if I had seen anything good.

"Just a gorgeous ocean view with a dolphin breaking the water, and then a midlife crisis lady sunbathing half-naked on her back lawn in front of a ton of landscapers."

"Oh, Brandon, cut the jokes."

"Sure thing," I said, not pushing the story. "Where are the girls?"

"Down the beach with Addison."

"I'm gonna go do some more work. Mind if I take off for a while? I'll leave the RV keys with you."

"Go ahead."

I CALLED Luke and got Marcy's home address from him. A few streets over from the beach, I found a small, rundown bungalow. The home must have been handed down to Marcy's mom from family as the plot of land was valuable due to its proximity to the beach, but the home itself was a complete teardown. I reached through a hole in the screen door and knocked on the front door, but no one answered. After a minute, I wandered around the side, where I found a woman with her head dropped in her right hand and a splinted left hand holding a lit cigarette. She had dark roots showing on her bleached blond hair, and her arms were covered in sleeved tattoos.

She heard me and looked up. "Who are you?"

"I'm friends with your father-in-law and your daughter. You're Cassie, right?"

"Depends who's asking."

"I'm a friend," I repeated. She didn't respond and

dropped her head back into her healthy hand again. "I know you're in trouble."

"I'm fine."

"No, you're not. You're working for a drug cartel and are crying because the vehicle you were driving was impounded. You're terrified someone's going to discover the drugs you had hidden on board."

"You a cop?"

"Nope. I said I'm a friend."

"I have no friends."

"I'd like to be one if you'll let me."

"What's your angle?" Cassie looked at me suspiciously. Then differently, like she was sizing me up. Like someone who saw a mark.

"No angle," I said, holding up my hands. I made sure my wedding band was front and center to make sure we were on the same page. "Mind if I sit down?"

She waved her hand. "Be my guest."

I sat down next to her. "My name's Brandon. Your father-in-law asked me to help as I know some people in government."

"Big deal."

I ignored the snide remark. "Your daughter has a bright future ahead of her. This isn't the life you want for her." There was a long pause. "Cassie?"

Cassie collected herself but started to cry before wiping her nose with the back of her arm. "When my husband passed away, I lost my north star."

I wanted to say that was a long time ago, and it was time to focus on Marcy. Instead, I forced out an, "I'm sorry for your loss."

"Life sucks, then you die, right?" she said.

"What's going to happen if you don't get that car back?"

"Then I'm as good as dead. They'll kill Marcy too."

"They're that ruthless?"

She nodded. "You have no idea. Cape Charles Customs is a front. They work for MS-13."

"I know."

"So you know what MS-13 are capable of?"

"Only what I read in the news."

"You have no idea. They've wiped out entire villages in South America that disobeyed them."

"I have some connections in government who might be able to—"

"This cartel owns half our government," Cassie huffed, looking at her watch. "Cape Charles Customs still think I'm on the way down to Miami. If I don't get that vehicle delivered to its buyer in the next twenty-four hours, I'm dead."

"How are you transporting the drugs?"

She looked at me with suspicion in her eyes.

I stood up and lifted my shirt, careful not to show the side with my appendix holster. "See, no wire." I took out my cell phone. "Look, I'll even power down my phone. You need to trust me, Cassie."

After I powered down the cell phone, Cassie seemed to relax ever so slightly. "They put the drugs into gas tanks so even trained drug dogs can't smell them. When I get the cars to the destination, they cut the tanks out, and there you go."

"The gas doesn't seep in and ruin the drugs—"

"The drugs are sealed in some sort of protective wrapping."

"Genius," I said. "So Cape Charles Customs is a complete front?"

"Yeah. All the antique cars they use are purchased on the Internet and completely refurbished. The only custom work they do is to install the drugs into the gas tanks. When we deliver the drugs, they just give the buyer the car along with the drugs. A thirty-grand antique Corvette is nothing when you're selling millions in drugs." She lit another cigarette.

I whistled. "That's serious money."

"Ha, Cape Charles is just a kiosk in a massive mall that spans the entire country, my friend. From what little I know, there are bigger distribution hubs throughout the country if you scratch the surface."

"How?"

"Rumor has it, individuals in government bring in entire planeloads of heroin from the Middle East and South America."

"You can prove this?"

Cassie shrugged her shoulders. "There's no getting out for me."

"How does Cape Charles Customs get the drugs here?"

"They come in by boat, I think."

"I need that information."

"They'll kill me and then my daughter."

"You said they'll kill her anyway." I paused and took a breath. "You want this life for her?"

Cassie started to cry again but somehow forced herself to stop. It reminded me of the strength and self-control I'd seen Marcy show. A moment later, Cassie tossed the cigarette into a rosebush. "Come inside."

I followed her through a side door into a kitchen that smelled of trash. There was a sink full of dirty dishes. Cassie moved a microwave aside and slid up a fake electric outlet cover to reveal a hidden spot. Inside the small space was jewelry, a roll of cash, and a thumb drive—which she removed.

"Come upstairs."

I followed Cassie through a messy living room that stunk of cigarettes, up a narrow stairwell to a large, sparse bedroom. The only photo on a dusty shelf was a black-and-white wedding picture of a gorgeous woman and a handsome young man in a military uniform. I leaned in to realize it wasn't some distant relative's wedding picture, but hers. Cassie was unrecognizable and looked like she had aged fifty years since that picture. She moved some items off a computer desk, emptied an ashtray into a plastic cup littered with other half-smoked cigarette butts and beer, and proceeded to spark up another cigarette. Cassie placed the thumb drive into an old computer with a 1990s block-shaped monitor. The machine whirred and clicked for a few minutes before the screen finally came to life. A single spreadsheet popped up. She clicked on it to reveal a page full of random numbers.

"I've never opened this before," she said, "and only saw it briefly when I downloaded it from Cape Charles's main computer."

"What is it?"

"I'm not sure," she said, "but it must be important. I think if you know some computer nerd in government, they might be able to decipher it, and maybe we could use it as leverage to save my life. I'm assuming it's bank accounts, or drug drop times, or something important."

"How'd you get this?"

"I had to sleep with two guys and wait until a third was passed out before I could access the computer to get it."

I stared at the page for long moments and tried to forget what she did to acquire the intel. "I have no idea what this is either, but I know people who can figure it out."

Cassie got up and walked around the room. I coughed from the smoke and smell. She politely put the cigarette out and opened a window. While I stared at the computer, Cassie sat on the edge of her bed and started to weep again.

"What am I going to do?"

My first thought was to panic. My family was scheduled to leave in two days. What could I do in that short a time? This woman was in crisis. "The local police and Coast Guard are off the table, I take it?"

"Some have been paid off," she cried. "Not all, but I don't know who is on the take. I know there are a ton of people on the federal level who are compromised as well, so be careful whom you approach for help. Cape Charles Customs may be small, but MS-13 is huge. Their motto is kill, rape, control, fear. Whoever helps us will need to relocate both me and Marcy, so don't hand this information over without getting something in return."

A door opened and closed beneath us. A minute later, Marcy came upstairs and found her mother wiping her eyes. "Brandon, what are you doing here? Mom, what's wrong?"

"Nothin', baby. Go get lunch started. I have a frozen pizza in the freezer."

"No, I want to know what's going on?"

"Nothing," Cassie raised her voice. "Just get lunch started so I can talk to Brandon about a few things."

"What do you need to talk to him about in your bedroom?"

I felt my face go flush as I pieced together Cassie's promiscuous past with how the situation must have looked to her highly intelligent daughter. I had to clear the air before it got too uncomfortable. "Your mom came clean with me. She wants to get out of the drug business, and we're reviewing a document of some sort on her computer."

"Brandon!" Cassie snapped. "Marcy doesn't need to know this."

"Sorry, but I don't want your daughter thinking something shady is going on. Besides, she's too smart to keep the truth from her."

Marcy came up behind me and stared at the computer screen.

"I know an IT guy back in South Boston who might be able to decipher this," I said.

"Move out of the way, you fossil," Marcy huffed.

I stood up and let Marcy sit on the chair. She stared at the numbers on the computer screen for long moments. I watched her eyes dart back and forth at a rapid pace. Like she was a robot processing data. "Mom, why didn't you ever show this to me?"

"I didn't think you could handle it—"

"That's just it. You didn't think!"

"Take a breath, Marcy," I said. "And take it down a notch. You're being disrespectful."

"Whatever," Marcy said. "How many times have you cleaned up after your mother wet her bed from being drunk, Brandon? My guess is a bit fat zero?"

Cassie dropped her head in her hands, defeated by a sixteen-year-old.

"She's still your mother," I said. "She's not a perfect mother, just like I'm not a perfect father."

"When you say not perfect, Brandon, do you mean Emily cleans your puke off the front steps of your house, too, when you come home drunk?"

"Stop it, Marcy!" Cassie said, clearly ashamed of being called out in front of a stranger.

"Enough!" I added.

Marcy waved us both away like we were beneath her. I could see her start to tear up as well as she recalled the painful memories. As intellectual as Marcy claimed to be, she was an emotional being like the rest of us. She bit her lip and seemed to refocus on the computer screen.

"If you had checked with me before, I would have told you those are lat-longitude coordinates."

"How'd you come to that conclusion?" I said, leaning down to stare at the screen. "The entire page is filled with numbers."

"Yeah, but there are only three negative numbers with decimal points," Marcy said. "Look. I bet the positive numbers that precede them are the latitude."

"And the rest of the numbers filling the page?"

"Are just static to confuse whoever might look at this."

After a long moment, I said, "Yeah, I was just about to say that."

Marcy gave what was a half-smile at my lame joke. I took out my phone and took a picture of the screen.

Cassie lit up another cigarette and blew smoke out the open window. "Could this be our get-out-of-jail card?"

"Maybe," I said. "We first need to find out where those coordinates are and possibly what's there. Well, Marcy, what do you think the coordinates are for?"

Marcy turned to her mom. "Drug drop-off or pickup locations?"

Cassie nodded and took another drag off her cigarette. Marcy opened a web page on the computer. The screen showed an hourglass as it waited to open the page. After a few seconds, Marcy huffed at the slow desktop computer's speed and took out her cell phone. She scrolled through a few pages. I asked what she was doing and was waved off again, like a student bothering their teacher with a question out of turn.

After a few minutes, Marcy said. "Odd."

"What?"

"I might be wrong after all. I thought these were lat-long coordinates, but if I mapped them correctly, they're in the middle of the Chesapeake Bay. I guess they could be meetup points for boats to swap the drugs, but that would seem like a highly visible target for Coast Guard, satellites, drones, or any recreational boats passing by. Maybe they do it in the dead of night, but still."

The dive sticker on the back of the diesel pickup truck at Cape Charles Customs flashed in my mind. "The coordinates are right, but I have a feeling it's not done on boats."

"I'm confused—"

"Same way they smuggle them in car gas tanks," I said. "In waterproof containers. They just sink them beneath the water."

"You think?"

"It's a stretch," I said. "But I have heard of drug cartels using semisubmersible vehicles. I saw a dive sticker on the back of a jacked-up truck in the parking lot of Cape Charles Customs the other day."

"That's Charlie's truck," Cassie said. "He's the big boss. Mean as a snake."

"Then the next step is we need to go to the library," Marcy said. "They have nautical maps of the Chesapeake Bay with depth charts."

"Are you sure you even need my help?" I joked.

"I'm going to take a shower," Cassie said. "I'll put the frozen pizza in the oven for when you two get back."

* * *

I TEXTED Annie to let her know to get lunch without me while Marcy and I walked a few blocks over to the library on Mason Avenue.

During the walk, I said, "You could be a little nicer to your mom."

"And she could grow up," Marcy snapped, her attitude returning in full force.

"She's still your mother."

"Giving birth doesn't make you a mother. It proves you're female."

A lot ran through my mind about how to respond. How some kids had it worse. How publicly shaming her mom didn't help. Rather than continue to argue, I simply replied, "I do see your point. I'm sorry for all that you've gone through, and all that you're going through."

Marcy exhaled, like she had been prepared for more arguing. "Thank you."

EIGHT

The library was an elegant granite building. It had a couple of small back rooms where we could spread out nautical maps of the Virginia coastline. Marcy took out her butterfly notebook and sharpened another number two pencil. I made several large photocopies of the Chesapeake Bay with depth and shoal grades for us to write on. One by one, we marked the coordinates from Cassie's document. They were three spots located under thirty feet of water where either a scuba diver or sub could place drugs in some sort of waterproof container. In that depth, scuba divers from Cape Charles Customs could easily pick up the package with a waiting boat above.

After we triple-checked the locations, Marcy said, "Now that we found the spots, what's next?"

"I have a friend in government who might be able to run with this intel."

"You can trust him?"

"Absolutely."

"Brandon, I'm trusting you with everything."

"And I've trusted him with everything on multiple occasions. Listen, if you have a better plan, then be my guest."

"No, sorry. I'm just a little nervous."

"The great Marcy Seabold gets nervous?"

"Oh, be quiet."

On the walk back to her house, I said, "When does your mom take her road trips?"

"Usually the last week of every month."

"Consistently?"

"Yes. That's the one thing she's consistent about."

"So that means the drugs are dropped off and retrieved the first few weeks of each month."

"That would make sense."

"We should be coming up on a drop-off or retrieval week then."

Annie texted that they were back at the beach from lunch, and she picked me up a sub. "I'm gonna meet my family for lunch. Want to join us?"

"Maybe I'll come down to hang out with you guys after I eat."

Back at the beach, Emily and Amber had taken Addison for a walk, and Annie was under the umbrella reading her book. I took up a chair next to her.

"How'd it go?" she said, handing me a turkey sandwich.

"Well, I'm moving in a direction as you suggested."

"Good," Annie said. "I found this adorable place we should go for dinner—"

Emily's cry interrupted the conversation. She rushed up the beach carrying Addison, saying something. In a flash, Annie and I were on our feet, rushing toward her. We reached her in seconds.

"What's wrong?" I asked. "Where's Amber?"

"Nothing's wrong," Emily panted, placing Addison in Annie's arms. "Look."

About twenty yards down the shoreline was Amber, dressed in a wrap and sun hat, facing a young, handsome male about her age. He was dressed in khaki shorts, a button-down shirt, and fancy sunglasses. They seemed deep in conversation and clearly knew one another. Suddenly the boy dropped to one knee and held up a small box in his hand.

"What's going on?"

"Oh my gosh," Annie gasped.

The dude opened the box, and even from our distance, everyone could see something big that sparkled. "Is that what I think it is?"

"Brandon," was all Annie said. Her tone implied I had asked a stupid question, and also to be quiet so she could process what was happening.

"They're so young," I added.

"Brandon!" This time my name was spoken with a tone that meant to be quiet with emphasis, so Annie could enjoy the moment. "She's twenty now."

I watched Amber place her hand to her mouth as this guy removed what some might consider a small meteorite from the jeweler's box.

"Can I go congratulate them?" Emily asked.

"No, sweetie," Annie said, holding her back.

"But—"

"Let Amber have her moment."

"What's taking so long?" I said, wondering what the beautiful couple were discussing. Either they were getting married, or they weren't.

"I don't know," Annie said. "We haven't even met this boy."

"Oh, now you're concerned?"

The guy tried to put the ring on her finger, but Amber withdrew. He stood up, the model boyfriend kissed her hand and spoke a bit more before he was allowed to finally place the ring on her finger. Amber held it up in the light. He kissed her cheek, and they walked back toward us, holding hands. Annie released Emily, who ran down the beach like a greyhound dog chasing a mechanical rabbit. My phone rang. It was Luke.

"I gotta take this."

"Brandon," this time, Annie's tone meant I was being rude.

"Just be a sec," I said, walking off before the couple reached us.

The moment I answered the phone, Luke shouted something inaudible. "Hold on. Slow down. I can't understand what you're saying. What's wrong?"

"Fire!?"

"Where are you?"

"At home," he said, taking a deep breath. "Marcy just called me. Her house is on fire."

I rushed toward the boardwalk pathway that led onto Bay Avenue. A spiral of smoke rose a few blocks away from the direction of Marcy's house. I started into a jog. "I'm on my way. Is Cassie in the house?"

"I have no idea," he said. "Marcy was frantic and just hung up. I'm leaving now. I'll meet you there."

By the time I made it to Marcy's house, a police cruiser and fire truck were onsite. Pedestrians lined the sidewalk. Even from fifty yards away, I could feel the heat of the fire. The entire house was engulfed. Another fire truck pulled up along with more police cars. I spotted Marcy sitting next to a police officer and called over to her. She told the officer to let me through the perimeter. I rushed over and fell to my knees at her level.

Marcy started talking fast. "I know Mom was in there. I just know it."

"Slow down, we don't know anything yet," I said, but in my gut, I felt that she was right.

A FEW MINUTES LATER, Luke's old F-150 pulled up. He rushed over, and Marcy collapsed into her grandfather's arms. He held it together for a good minute before he broke down as well. The three of us sat off to the side near a patrol car to watch the bonfire like it was some Viking funeral pyre. The second fire truck had given up on Marcy's house and now doused the closest neighbor's house with water to keep it from igniting. I texted Annie to let her know what had happened, that I'd be with Luke and Marcy for the rest of the day, and would catch up with them later.

Above, the blazing sun added to the deathly heat. EMTs brought us bottles of water, and a police officer took Marcy's statement. Even in this condition, she was self-aware not to give away too much. She said I was a friend of the family who was at the beach, and Luke was her grandfather who lived nearby. When Marcy asked the officer if anyone thought there was foul play, he just shrugged and said he didn't know, but that the fire department would do an investigation.

Marcy kept calling her mom's cell phone, but it went directly to voicemail. Marcy hung on to her grandfather's arm like it was a lifeline. If Cassie was in the house, then Luke was Marcy's last surviving relative. I felt sad for the small world that was closing in around this young girl. She desperately needed to know that she had a Father in Heaven that loved her, especially during a time like this.

* * *

IT WASN'T until around eight o'clock in the evening, after the fire was completely out, when a somber firefighter approached us. He removed his helmet the way a cowboy would take off his hat when entering someone's home. He rested the helmet over his heart and stood in front of the three of us. Soot caked his face, and he looked both exhausted and distraught.

"You found her," Marcy said.

"We found someone," the firefighter said just above a whisper. "We can't be sure it was your mom—"

Marcy got up and started toward the remains of the house. "I have to see. She's missing a tooth in the back of her mouth, and I can tell by her tattoos—"

The firefighter caught her and looked at me with pleading eyes. "She's in no condition to view this scene."

"I can too," Marcy said. "Let go of me."

I rested my hand on Marcy's shoulder. She turned around and collapsed in my arms, weeping uncontrollably. Luke stood there stoic, as if he were reliving some nightmare from his past. Maybe the death of his son? After a minute, he joined us in a group hug.

* * *

IT WAS around midnight when Luke and I finally got Marcy to go to sleep in her bedroom upstairs at his farmhouse. Luke and I sat across from one another at his small kitchen table with cups of tea like we had the first night we met. Those first cups of tea were during a dark time and a scary situation. This time wasn't much different.

"What do you think, Brandon?"

"I'm not one for conspiracies, but I'm also not one for coincidences."

I filled Luke in on what had transpired with my conversation with Cassie, and how she had been moving drugs up and down the coast in the antique cars. I went on to explain the thumb drive Cassie had, and how Marcy broke the code. Luke closed his eyes and shook his head in what appeared to be disappointment. A moment later, he gave a slight smirk. I knew exactly what he was thinking. He was impressed, even proud, of his granddaughter's genius at figuring this all out.

"She was right all along," I said.

"Told you my granddaughter was special."

"She's special, all right."

"Do you think they found out Cassie's car was impounded and killed her?" Luke asked.

I shrugged. "Either that, or maybe there was some sort of software worm that alerted people to the document being opened on her home computer? I don't know enough about computer programming to know for sure."

"What are we going to do?"

"I'm gonna pray about it and sleep on it, and we'll talk in the morning?"

"Me too." Before I left, Luke added. "I'm glad you're here, Brandon."

"I still don't know what I can do," I said, "but I promise you it won't be for lack of trying."

* * *

BACK AT THE GUESTHOUSE, everyone was asleep except Annie. I had texted her throughout the night to keep her updated.

"How's Marcy?"

"A mess," I said, sliding into bed next to her. "She's a tough girl, though."

"But she's still just a girl," Annie said. "So, what are you going to do?"

"I'm gonna start kicking over some rocks to see what I find, but what would you think about you guys going home first thing tomorrow?"

"Why? Do you think it's dangerous here?"

I nodded. "It was probably arson, and the body is probably Cassie, which means murder."

"Which means?"

"I'm not convinced they won't come after Marcy or Luke if they think Cassie talked before she died. It won't be hard to figure out where the daughter is staying."

"How will you get home?"

"Rent a car."

"I don't like the idea of you staying here to deal with this."

"You said to help."

Annie pursed her lips. "You know what I meant. This is too big for you."

"I can do all things through Christ who strengthens me," I said, picking up my travel Bible. "Now I gotta figure out a game plan, and the only way to do that is to speak with the Boss."

Annie kissed me on the cheek and rolled over with an "I love you."

I spent the next hour praying and searching scripture for guidance. I scoured the Bible looking for clarity, messages, anything that showed God giving answers when people needed one. I found nothing that stuck out. I came away from my prayer time, convinced I was going to have to be patient for His plan to unfold in His time. The last image before I fell asleep was of my new friend, Charles Coyne. His studies on patience seemed to be a lesson meant for me.

* * *

After a fitful night's sleep, I was up before everyone else the next morning. I texted Drake, asking him to call me when he had a chance. Next, I went into town and picked up an iced coffee and bagels at the coffee shop to bring back. Charles Coyne was at his normal table upstairs. He was dressed in his bow tie and dress shirt, along with an open Bible.

"Good morning, Charles," I said, walking up the stairs.

"Good morning, Mr. Hall. How are things?"

"Been better."

"Did yesterday's fire have anything to do with what you're dealing with?" I nodded. "Are you going to get involved?"

"I believe I already am. I just don't know what to do next."

"There are answers to your questions if you want them. Those who seek, find. Knock, and it shall be opened."

"You're no help with vague references."

Charles got up and placed his Bible in his leather briefcase. "Walk with me."

Outside, I left the bagels in the RV and walked with Charles along Mason Avenue. I couldn't place his age as he walked like a young man, but was clearly in his late sixties or early seventies. He was taller than me, at least six foot three, and fit, but not muscular.

"Tell me what your thoughts are," I said.

"Local police can't be trusted."

"How sure are you?"

"People have reported strange things surrounding Cape Charles Customs to the police, and nothing ever comes from it."

"What about Coast Guard?"

"Same."

"And so you've just been sitting around and what, waiting—"

"And praying."

"For?"

"For you to show up," he said. "And the Lord is faithful."

"Will you stop it with the, I'm an answer to prayer stuff, Charles?"

"I think you are." He momentarily stopped to poke me in the arm before mumbling a "Hmm."

"What was that?"

"Just checking again on Hebrews 13:2," he said.

"Be not forgetful to entertain strangers: for thereby some have entertained angels unawares," I said. "Trust me. I'm no angel."

"Well, at a minimum, you're an answer to prayer."

"Regardless of what you think, I'm at a loss as to what to do."

"What do you know so far?"

"Woman who died yesterday was running drugs for Cape Charles Customs. From what I know, they're a subsidiary of MS-13 and run at least a portion of their US Eastern Seaboard operations. Mom had a get-out-of-jail card and ended up dead."

"The get out of jail card?"

"Not sure yet." I didn't mention Marcy or Luke's names, or that we thought the coding was drop-off points for drugs. Not sure why. I trusted Charles, but I still only just met him. "This needs to get bumped up the chain to someone with greater authority and power."

"I bumped it up to the highest authority," he said, "and I have good reason to believe you're here to fix this."

I ignored the comment. "I have a friend in government who may be able to take this off my plate."

"You can trust him?"

"With my life," I said. "Problem is, he's on a mission."

We stopped outside a real estate office, and Charles turned around to walk us back toward the RV. "What other data do you have?"

"A few loose leads," I said.

"You need to just put one foot in front of the other," he said. "Walk in faith, and God will open doors."

We reached the RV. "Well, my friend, I'll be praying for you."

"Thanks," I said, getting into the RV. A minute later, I drove down Mason Avenue and slowed down to the pace Charles walked. He clearly saw me but didn't turn his head. "By the way, what were you reading this morning?"

"The Psalms," he said, holding his hands up toward Heaven. "Psalm 77:19. Thy way is in the sea, and Thy path in the great waters, and Thy footsteps are not known."

"Fitting for our location," I said.

NINE

On the drive back to the guesthouse, I prayed about what steps to take next. No local law enforcement could be trusted, Cassie was more than likely dead, and Marcy and Luke's safety was up in the air. I needed Roger Drake now more than ever, but that idea was more dream than reality. He was MIA in Antarctica somewhere and wouldn't be back for weeks. I was on my own and had to do something with what little I had. Charles Coyne's Bible verse floated back into my consciousness. Thy way is in the sea, and Thy path in the great waters. An idea started to take shape.

Back at the guesthouse, I delivered the bad news along with breakfast. Between the shark attacks and the excitement surrounding Marcy and Luke, my wife was ready to go home. Emily was bummed, and Amber seemed indifferent. Her mind was clearly on other things. I sat down across from her as she ate a bagel and stared at the massive ring on her left hand.

"A penny for your thoughts? Or, in your case, forty-five grand for your thoughts?"

Amber chuckled, holding the stone higher so the center solitaire's surrounding diamonds caught the sunlight through the window. "It is a bit gaudy, but I do like it."

"I liked Brad."

"It was Brian," Amber giggled. "And you only met him once, and he wanted to get married like a month into our relationship. Steve and I have been dating for a while."

"I would like to meet this Steve."

"You're gonna like him," Emily said from the living room. "He hung out at the beach with us all afternoon."

I turned to Annie, who said, "He's very charming."

"You're okay with our girl here being married so young?"

"She's her own woman."

"She's barely out of diapers," I said, ignoring the fact Amber sat across from me.

Annie came up and hugged Amber. "She's got a brilliant mind."

"I know she does," I said. "But intellect, maturity, and wisdom are sometimes mutually exclusive."

I suddenly realized this was almost a mirror image of the conversation I had with Marcy. I turned to Amber, hoping one of my comments would spark a response, but she seemed to enjoy the banter of Annie and me arguing over her. It was as if she relished the thought of two loving parents worried about her.

Amber reached over and touched my hand. "Don't worry, I told Steve I want a long engagement."

"I don't care if it's long or short," I said. "I just want you to be sure."

"We love you," Annie said.

"Just be sure," I repeated. "Like Annie said. We love you."

Amber teared up and nodded as if to say she loved us too.

* * *

AN HOUR LATER, the large items were packed into the RV. I removed my scuba gear and go bag, which held extra magazines for my pistol as well as a myriad of other items I may need were I to run into trouble. As the girls loaded up the last of the smaller items, I wandered over to Luke's house. Marcy and Luke sat outside. The poor girl was slumped down in an Adirondack chair with a full smoothie in front of her. Luke sat with a cowboy hat on, coffee in hand, watching her like a hawk. As if, at any moment, she might run away.

"You're leaving," Marcy said without turning her head.

"No, I'm sending my family home, and I'm staying."

Marcy nearly jumped out of her seat. "Really?" She started talking super quickly, like she had ten cups of coffee. "I really appreciate it, Brandon. I know how we can get back at them. First, I want to torch Cape Charles Customs and—"

"Hold on a second," I interrupted. "First, no one is torching anything. Second, I think we need to have a talk about you two possibly leaving the property for a few days. Maybe staying in a motel?"

"I ain't leaving," Luke said.

"And neither am I," Marcy added. "I'm not afraid. I want those bastards to pay for what they did."

"Language, young lady," Luke corrected her.

"Vengeance is the Lord's," I said.

"Amen," Luke added.

"Where was God when Mom was murdered?"

"We don't know—"

Marcy sat back down and folded her arms. "Seriously? You think the house randomly caught fire? You think that body is some random stranger, and Mom is where? Been on a shopping binge for the past twenty-four hours?"

I shook my head. "No, Marcy. I don't. I believe you now. I believe that Cape Charles Customs is selling drugs. I believe they are connected to MS-13. I believe pretty much everything you said from start to finish." I sat down next to her. "And I do believe that was your mom."

"Well, in case you didn't believe me, I kind of hacked into the fire department's computer system last night."

"You did not!"

"Just a little," she said, holding up her thumb and index finger slightly apart.

"Marcy, that's like saying you committed a little bit of a felony."

"It wasn't hard." She took out her cell phone and started to read. "I found a preliminary report stating they found bruising on the neck of the victim. The fire accelerant was grease on the stove, which caught a dish-towel hanging above it." Before I could say anything, she added, "You were there. You heard Mom say she was putting a frozen pizza in the oven. The grease fire was made to look like an accident."

"Maybe she changed her mind?" Luke said.

"And the bruising on her neck? She was strangled. Murdered, Grampy!"

"You're right," he confessed.

Marcy collected herself. "So, what are your thoughts, Brandon?"

I said one final silent prayer. There only seemed to be one option in front of me. "Luke, I need to borrow your boat."

"I'm not tracking with you, Brandon?"

"I brought a scuba tank on the off chance I might do a recreational dive with someone from a local dive shop."

"We're going after the drugs!" Marcy said.

"What's this we stuff?"

"You shouldn't dive alone, so I'm at least going to be on the boat as a backup in case anything happens."

"Absolutely not," Luke said. "I'll take Brandon out."

"Fine," Marcy huffed, "I'll just wait here by myself on the farm. Probably the least safe place for me to be, but go ahead."

"I'll let you two figure this one out," I said. "I'm gonna go get my family on the road. I'll be back in a few hours."

* * *

Back at the guesthouse, everyone was loaded up into the RV. It took us an hour to get back over to the mainland, where we found a car rental place in Virginia Beach. The last time I had driven through it was nearing winter. The beach had been empty, and I was on the run with a fugitive. Now, it was over ninety degrees, people were everywhere in shorts and tank tops, and the beach was covered in umbrellas. The only rental car available was a small four-door compact car from a shady dealership on a sketchy side street. For lunch, we stopped at a small clam shack and spent a half hour afterward walking around shops along the beach. All too soon, I handed the RV keys over to Annie and kissed the girls.

"Do you have all your things out of the RV?"

I nodded. "I brought khaki pants and a dress shirt, but I'm gonna find a shop and pick up a tie in case I'm still here by the time they hold a service for Marcy's mom."

"I don't want you here longer than a couple of days," Annie said. "I'll be praying for you."

"Daddy, please come home with us," Emily said from the back seat.

"I need to help out Luke and Marcy for a few days, sweetie. It's the right thing to do."

"I guess."

"Amber, keep an eye on everyone, and don't run off getting married until I get back."

"Don't worry," she laughed. "Be safe and come home soon."

"God willing."

Through the window, I blew Addison a kiss, who simply held up her hand and said, "Dadda!"

Together, we prayed for safe travels before I watched them drive off like they were heading to Montana rather than back to Halifax County, just a few hours away. I had no idea what lay in front of me, but somehow I knew danger was going to be involved. This wasn't some street gang. MS-13 was a well-oiled machine with near-infinite resources.

A quick search on my cell phone located a consignment store where I found a tie and sports jacket for thirteen bucks. Before driving back to Cape Charles, I texted

Roger Drake again. I told him that I had a problem that needed someone of his caliber. Still no response. Back at the farm, Luke and Marcy waited outside the guesthouse in the Adirondack chairs sipping sweet tea. Behind them was Luke's old Ford pickup. Attached to the bumper hitch was a trailer with the wooden Starcraft boat.

The moment I stepped out of the car, Marcy said, "We're ready."

I took out one of the wrinkled maps that Marcy and I had charted in the library and spread it out on the hood of the rental car. The closest of the three lat-long coordinates was a spot between Cape Charles and Kiptopeke State Park near the mouth of the Chesapeake Bay.

"I'm going to dive down to this first location," I said, pointing to the map, "and see if there's a load of drugs waiting to be picked up."

"And if there is?" Luke said.

"Then I'm going to take it."

"And do what with it?"

"Wait until my contact in government gets back from his mission and hand it off to him. I trust this guy, and he's connected with all the patriots in government. He'll get it into the right hands in DEA and get this taken care of."

"Sounds like a plan," Luke said.

"Marcy, you want justice for your mom, this is it. We may also need this as leverage. If MS-13 targets you two before my friends get here."

"Why would they do that?" Luke said.

"If they think Cassie talked," I said, "then your lives could be in danger. They won't want any loose ends."

Luke pulled Marcy close. "What a wicked organization."

"The more plausible scenario is that we get the drugs.

Hand them off to my friends, and it will make things go a lot quicker if you need to be relocated or given new identities."

"Then what are we waiting for?" Marcy said.

"Hold on a sec," I said. "This isn't a team sport. I don't want to have to worry about you guys while I'm out there."

"Brandon, you're taking a forty-year-old wooden boat with a fifty-year-old outboard motor out on the Chesapeake Bay," Luke said. "These are waters you're not familiar with. I'm going to need to be there to guide you and deal with any quirks that come up with the engine."

"And there's no way you're leaving me here alone," Marcy added.

Marcy was right. She was safer with us than home alone, so I agreed. A half-hour later, my gear was on board the boat, and the three of us were crammed into Luke's single-cab old Ford pickup. The truck towed the old boat through Cape Charles with creaks and groans. On a side street was a bed and breakfast with a familiar lowrider pickup truck parked out front. Two men spoke to one another in front of the truck.

"Luke, slow down but don't stop."

As we drove by, the men looked over at us, but I had on sunglasses with the window up. I could see the Steve kid who proposed to Amber talking with another muscular guy I didn't recognize. If the other guy was the one who owned the truck, then his name was Stanwick, who went by Romeo. The hired muscle Amber's cousin used for his shady business dealings.

"Recognize someone?"

"Possibly," I said. "A problem I'm gonna have to table for now."

* * *

We reached the boat ramp and had to wait in the queue for a half hour as fancier trucks towing fancier boats launched in front of us. When it was our turn, people stared at the old boat and truck like we were a bunch of rednecks dressed in camo showing up for dinner at the Four Seasons. I ignored the attention and backed the truck down to the water while Luke took the boat off the trailer. After parking the truck, Luke took us out into the channel with a putt-putt from the stern bench of the antique Evinrude outboard. I used my phone to guide us to the coordinates. We passed by Kiptopeke State Park, where the shadowed hulls of half-submerged cargo ships lay a couple of hundred yards offshore.

Before I could ask, Luke said, "Those are nine World War II boats the state of Virginia sunk to protect the pier and coastline, which act as a surf break."

I looked at the sad, tattered remains of the boats that may have transported soldiers, or cargo, over to Europe eighty years ago. They were broken yet pretty at the same time. There was something different about them I couldn't place, though.

"They're made of concrete," Luke said.

"You're kidding?"

"It's true," Marcy said.

"We had a shortage of metal during the war, so they were built out of concrete."

"I guess if you displace the right amount of water and factor in mass, gravity, and buoyancy, it doesn't matter what the boat is made of."

"It's called the Archimedes' principle," Marcy added.

I widened my eyes as if Marcy had just spoken ancient Egyptian. "Yeah, exactly what I was thinking."

Luke smiled from the stern bench as if he was used to his granddaughter spouting off facts like this. "The entire war effort was creative," he added. "Everyone pitched in back then. My uncle came home early with an injury and still collected metal for the cause."

I shook my head. "I can't ever imagine our country being that united again."

We soon left the antique boats in the distance and found our spot. On the surface, there was nothing special about the area. No markers or buoys. However, the underwater chart showed a small ledge with a drop-off surrounding it. A perfect plateau for a drug drop point. It took me a few minutes to put on my three-millimeter wetsuit and gear.

Luke was about to drop the anchor, but I grabbed his hand. "I don't want to disturb anything beneath us until I see what's down there first."

"What are you thinking?"

"Booby traps," Marcy said.

"You never know," I said.

"Current is pretty strong, Brandon."

I thought for a minute. "After I'm in, go about twenty yards over there and drop anchor."

"Roger that."

Dark clouds overshadowed the sun, as if to remind me to take a flashlight. Along with my dive knife, I also brought a pry bar and adjustable wrench, which I attached to a belt. I dropped over the side and floated for a minute, checking my buoyancy control device and regulator. I gave a thumbs-up and released the air from the BCD, allowing me to descend beneath the surface. Above, the outboard motor moved off with a smoother sound underwater than it made above.

The water, like the Dan River, was murky. The result of an influx of freshwater and clay from the Chesapeake mixing with the sea. Around fifteen feet, I pressurized my ears and continued down to eighteen feet. From what I could see, it was a mirror image of the chart with a sandy platform and sheer drop-offs all around. I swam around until I found the first man-made thing. A fishing net with rotted fish still inside caught on a line attached to a cement platform. I followed the line down to the platform and pulled out the flashlight, which did little to cut through the murkiness.

On the platform was what looked like a plastic piece of luggage about three feet square complete with a handle on it. It lay on its side and had a thin wire attached to a bolt on the platform. Around the outside of the suitcase was an old dive belt used to weigh it down. I unlatched the belt allowing the suitcase to move about on the sandy floor before catching on the safety wire. With a few tries from the pry bar, I popped the bolt from the cement pad and freed the suitcase.

Suddenly, I was hit from behind. Something, or someone, had bumped into my tank. I turned around but saw nothing. Could it have been my imagination? To the right, something flashed, like a camera going off. Could MS-13 set up motion detection cameras? Then it occurred to me that it could be some sort of booby trap. Upon closer inspection, I found a small stainless box about ten feet over from the suitcase. About every eight seconds, light flashed from the metal box. There did not seem to be any photo lens, though. I put the flashlight away and touched the device while holding onto the suitcase. It wasn't bolted to the pad as it was heavy enough to be weighted down. I lifted the device into the crook of my arm with the suitcase and, with my free hand, inflated my BCD, but something slammed into my tank again. This time was hard, and this time it wasn't my imagination.

I swung around to see the shape of a six-foot shark move off into the darkness. No idea what species, but it was clearly being aggressive. I nearly spit the regulator out of my mouth. I had never encountered a shark this big in the wild before. Fight-or-flight kicked in, with flight winning. I needed to get to the surface and would figure out the electronic device later. I restarted my ascent, but got entangled in the fishing net. I pushed it aside. The electronic device flashed again and seemed to spark a thought. It wasn't an old fishing net randomly caught on the platform, but a massive chum bag deliberately tethered to the cement platform. A device used to attract sharks, so they would act as guard dogs for the drugs.

Something rubbed up against my fin. I looked down to find a three-foot shark swimming between my legs. I started to hyperventilate and almost let go of the drugs and metal box so I could swim faster. More sharks surrounded me. Every fear was compounded by the fact that I could not see more than a few feet. I held the suitcase in front like a shield as I moved off from the chum bag, but the sharks seemed to follow me like I was a meaty bone. I punched my BCD, pumped my fins, and continued the ascent.

Another shark approached head-on. It was a bull shark. One of the nastiest sharks in the wild when it comes to attacking humans. My heart beat so hard I thought it was going to explode. I used the suitcase to bump its nose and push it away. The animal was not happy with the gesture. At this point, everywhere I turned, I saw fins.

Something hit my tank again, and I screamed and almost spat out my regulator. Throughout this panic, I heard a small, quiet voice that, for the life of me, seemed to have a Cajun accent.

"Let go."

TEN

Let go of what? The drugs? No matter where I turned, I was in the middle of a whirlwind of fins. Something about me was attracting the sharks. Causing a feeding frenzy-like situation, but there was no blood to attract the animals. Something else was causing the hysteria. It had to be something in the suitcase, or the flashing metal box. I chose to let go of the electronic device. The sharks tore off after it like a cat chasing a mouse. By the time I reached the surface, Luke had seen my bubbles and moved the boat nearby. Without me saying a word Luke and Marcy somehow knew to help me out of the water as quickly as possible. I handed them the suitcase and nearly jumped out of the water and onto the boat.

Once on the boat deck, they started to pepper me with questions, but I didn't speak for a few minutes as I removed the tank and fins before finally sitting down and catching my breath.

Finally, I said, "Sharks. Lots of them."

"Oh my gosh," Marcy said. "Are you okay?"

"I think I wet my wetsuit. Otherwise, praise God I'm whole."

I got up and looked around as if we were being watched. "Let's get out of here."

On the way back to Cape Charles, I explained about the electronic device and chum bag. "Both items must have been put in place to attract the sharks so they'd act like security guards around the drugs. The chum bag being a backup to the electronic device."

"That's pretty creative," Marcy said. "I've read about technology the Navy developed to repel sharks, but never to attract them."

"Most sharks are harmless," Luke said, clearly trying to make me feel better.

"These weren't harmless," I said. "I think most of them were bull sharks too."

"Brandon's right, Grampy," Marcy said. "Where we are in the Chesapeake Bay is where a lot of freshwater meets saltwater, and bull sharks can swim up rivers in both salt and fresh water."

I used the pry bar to work on the suitcase while Luke drove the boat, and Marcy continued to add to my panic by reading bull shark statistics from her cell phone. "They have one of the highest concentrations of testosterone of any animal on the planet and account for being in the top three shark species that attack humans."

"Marcy, can we talk about something else please?" I asked.

"Oh, sure. Sorry."

After a few minutes, I was able to open the suitcase a few inches. Enough to jam the pry bar in between the small gap.

"Shouldn't we wait until we're home?" Luke asked from the driver's seat.

"Negative," I said. "If there's a gazillion dollars worth of drugs in here, there very well could be a tracking device inside as well. Marcy, stand near the bow."

"Why."

I placed my mask back on. "It could also be booby-trapped."

Finally, the seal broke, and the two pieces popped apart with no issues. Inside were bags of double-sealed white powder.

Marcy peered over. "What is it?"

"I'm assuming some type of heroin," I said, removing my mask. "And judging by the weight of the suitcase, we've got about well over a hundred pounds of the stuff."

"Wonder what it's worth?"

"No idea."

"I don't like the fact that we're gonna hold onto this," Luke said.

"Would you rather this make it onto the street?" I asked, removing the bags from inside.

I transferred the bags into a large haversack. I used a half cinder block Luke kept on board as an anchor for lobster pots, which I placed back in the briefcase. A zip tie closed it back together, and a moment later, the empty suitcase was on its way back to the bottom of the Chesapeake Bay just in case there was a GPS device built into the casing.

* * *

IT WAS sunset by the time we pulled the truck and boat back into the farm. I was famished and exhausted. Luke made us bacon and eggs for dinner. There was a message on Luke's answering machine to call a Sergeant Cox.

Marcy and I sat at the kitchen table while Luke returned the call.

"Cox," I said, turning to Marcy.

Marcy whispered, "That's the cop whose email I found in Jeremy's cell phone mentioning Cape Charles Customs."

"Remind me to tell you about his house," I whispered back.

Luke didn't talk much on the phone call. Only a "Yes, sir," and "I understand."

After he got off the phone, Marcy asked, "What's the deal, Grampy?"

"Police officer claims your mom passed from inhalation and that there was no foul play."

"That's utter crap!" Marcy stood up and was about to throw a glass of milk across the room. I snatched it from her hand just in time. Instead, she swung at the air and shouted in what sounded like a primordial scream of both anger and frustration.

"I hate them," she shouted. "I hate them all!"

Marcy fell back into her seat and dropped her head in her hands, sobbing. The day's distraction was gone. She was back to the raw reality that her mom had been murdered, which was compounded by the fact that some of the local authorities were helping to cover it up.

"Luke, you did the right thing by not pushing back," I said. "The last thing we should do is let them think we suspect anything."

Luke nodded. "Ignorance is a form of protection."

"I won't let them get away with this," Marcy sniffled from her forward position.

"We're not going to," I promised.

My cell phone rang. It came up as an unknown

number, which meant it was spam, or Roger Drake. "Brandon Hall speaking?"

There was a crackling of static before Drake's smooth voice came over the line. "What trouble did you get yourself into now, boy?"

"Where are you?"

"Stuck in the Falkland Islands," he said. "Mission is gonna be scrubbed if the weather doesn't break."

I didn't bother to step outside. "I'm staring at what looks like about a hundred and fifty or so pounds of some form of heroin, I think."

"And what did you do to come across this?"

I told him about Marcy, Luke, and Cassie. About Cassie's job for Cape Charles Customs. The company's ties to MS-13 and the fact that no authorities in the area could be trusted, including some Coast Guard and police. About Cassie's murder and the thumb drive she smuggled out of Cape Charles Customs, which had the coordinates to the three dive spots.

"This is why I pray for you even when you're on the farm," Drake exhaled. "Expecting you to go on vacation and relax is like asking a fox to relax in a henhouse. Nothing but trouble is what happens. And you say you dove down to get this package?"

"Yeah."

"We've known of cartels using semisubmersible vehicles, but underwater drop-offs are a new thing. You said there are two more drop-off points you haven't been to yet. Do you think you can retrieve those packages in the next day or two?"

"I do, but speaking of that," I said. "Do you have access to gear you could send me?"

"Whatever you need short of an F-35 fighter, I can get you within eighteen hours. Just give me an address."

I walked outside to look at the address number on Luke's house. "I ran into some trouble while diving."

"Who, you?" Drake said, dripping with sarcasm.

"They set up a chum bag and some sort of electronic device to attract sharks. I think it acted like a homing beacon of sorts."

"Interesting. So the sharks acted as sentries to guard the drugs?"

"Yeah. I'm assuming they can remotely shut down the device before diving down to retrieve the drugs."

"We now have the technology to make wearable shark-repelling devices," Drake said. "They're the size of a wristwatch and use a magnetic field to repel the animals." He paused for a moment. "Theoretically, if scientists discovered frequencies to repel the animals, I don't see why you couldn't find frequencies to attract the animals as well."

"Well, it's genius," I said, "and scary."

"Did you recover the device?"

"I dropped it. Sorry."

"So what do you need?"

"I need dive chainmail for shark protection, a speargun, a shark stick, and while you're at it, send me one of those high-tech repelling electronic devices you just mentioned."

"Hold on, I'm writing this down."

"I knew MS-13 was heavily funded," I said, "but I'm still just shocked at how high-tech they are."

"This isn't some drug den in a jungle pushing marijuana out on donkeys, son. They have more technology than most governments. We have reason to believe MS-13 has its own satellite in orbit." After a few moments, Drake said, "What else?"

"Not sure."

"I can't be there right now, so the sky's the limit. I want you to go worst-case scenario."

"As in?"

"As in, you get caught with your hand in the cookie jar, and a firefight ensues."

"Well," I thought for a moment. "Then I could use a shotgun with fifty rounds of double 00 buck and fifty slugs."

"Fine," Drake said, "but this is MS-13, not skeet shooting at the country club."

I thought for a moment. It was hard for me to put on a tinfoil hat, even after all I had been through over the past few years. "How about an AR-10 with two hundred rounds of .308 and six mags? A plated chest rig with a KA-BAR fixed blade and an IFAK. Might as well throw in a Kevlar blanket."

Drake didn't balk at any of it. "Helmet and night vision?"

"Oh yeah, duh. Yes, please."

"I'll throw in some MREs and a Glock 17," Drake said. "What else?"

"I can't think of anything else."

"It'll be there before you wake up tomorrow morning."

I gave Drake the address and hung up. When I turned around, Marcy was standing in the doorway with Luke behind her.

Luke cleared his throat. "You preparing for war, Brandon?"

"He's preparing for anything," Marcy added.

"Conflict is a last resort," I said. "But better to have and not need, than to need and not have."

"Well, I hope it doesn't come to that," Luke said.

"I don't," Marcy huffed.

I went to Marcy. "I can't begin to understand what it's like to lose your dad and then your mom this way, but I do know what it's like to hold on to anger. It's like drinking poison and hoping the other person will get sick."

"What could you know about holding on to anger? You're Mr. Perfect."

"I lost my infant son in a car wreck." I shut my eyes, trying to block out the images that had been seared into my mind like a branding. "It took years, but I confronted the drunk driver responsible for his death and forgave him."

"It's the only thing keeping me going right now, Brandon. If I let go—" she caught herself. "I'll fall apart."

I turned to Luke. The old man just shrugged his shoulders. I wanted to quote what the Bible said about praying for your enemies, but Marcy wouldn't understand. Instead, I said, "Even our enemies are Imago Dei."

"Image bearers of God," Marcy translated.

Her intellect still caught me off guard. "Yes. Image bearers who chose to pursue evil but could still be saved if they would only believe in Jesus."

"If what you say is true, then my hope is that they choose never to believe. If Hell exists, I want these people to burn in it forever."

Marcy was getting more worked up, so I decided to change the subject. "What say we order pizza?"

"I'm paying," Luke said. "It's the least I can do for what you're putting up with."

"Nonsense," I said. "You're gonna give me a discount on next summer's rental?"

"Discount?" Luke chuckled. "Your family can stay the entire summer if you want."

I placed the duffle bag next to my suitcase in the

small living room. The couch was old but comfortable. Better than anything I had slept on in the Marines. "I'm gonna crash in here tonight if that's okay?"

"Marcy sleeps in her dad's old bedroom upstairs," Luke said, "and mine is next to hers. We do have a small third bedroom I've used as an office if you want—"

"Couch is fine," I said. "I want to stand guard."

"Just in case?"

"You never know," I said.

* * *

AFTER DINNER, we all agreed to go to bed early. The next day was going to be long. I had two dives to do with potential shark attacks involved.

My sleep was fitful that night. Images of dark waters and fins haunted me. I awoke covered in sweat, fearing the dives I knew had to be done in a few short hours. Unlike what I had previously told my family about the low probability of shark attacks, I knew the percentages were now high due to the chum bags and electronic devices. If Roger Drake came through, I'd have chain-mail, an electronic deterrent, along with a speargun and shark stick, which was a shotgun shell mounted on the end of a loaded baton. Still, none of it was a guarantee, and the murkiness of the Chesapeake Bay added to the haunting picture. I prayed until my heart calmed but was unable to recapture sleep.

* * *

EARLY THE NEXT MORNING, we ate a bland breakfast of toast, eggs, and coffee. I had no appetite but forced myself to eat something as I'd need the calories for the work ahead. Marcy packed lunches and bottles of water for us. An hour later, a blacked out SUV pulled up in front of the farmhouse. A young Navy male stepped out wearing BDU fatigues and wraparound sunglasses.

"Morning, sir," the young man said, opening the tailgate of the SUV. "You Mr. Hall?"

"That's me."

"Got some gear for you."

He unloaded the first of three duffle bags.

"Do I need to sign anything?"

"Negative," he said, placing the last bag on the ground. A moment later, he got in the SUV and drove off.

I unzipped the bags. Everything I asked for as there. All weapons and ammo were in one bag wrapped in the Kevlar blanket. This included the speargun and shark stick. The chest rig, IFAK, and helmet were in another bag, along with the chainmail suit. I held up the thin mesh suit, sunlight seeped through the shiny stainless-steel circlets almost the way blood might pour through. I pushed the thought, and the suit, away. With all the scuba-related gear loaded on Luke's boat, I locked the rest of the gear into the rental car's trunk.

* * *

AT THE BOAT LAUNCH, we repeated the same procedure, but this time I ran the boat while Luke backed the truck into the water. I wanted to familiarize myself with the boat in case I needed to take it out myself. Luke had instructed me on how to throttle up the engine without stalling, and how to start it back up without flooding the engine. I drove us out into the channel, and we swapped off after a half-hour so I could familiarize myself with some of the new gear. I put together the shark bangstick, which was a one-shot option. It was a metal baton with a single shot of varying calibers at the end. This one was fitted for a twelve-gauge shell. You load the single shell at the head, and if needed, slam it into a shark, and boom. The defensive weapon was a close-quarter one-shot option and would have to be reloaded on the surface. The speargun was also a one-shot option but allowed the user a distance shot. The speargun carried an extra bolt and could be reloaded underwater. The ankle bracelet looked like an oversized smartwatch. I couldn't imagine it would do anything, but I was happy to have it.

It took us a half-hour to get to the second drug drop point on the map. This one was off of Eastville. There was nothing special about this location except that it seemed to be out of the way. There were no lobster buoys around, and it was in a spot that seemed to be devoid of boat traffic. We anchored right over the lat-long mark this time. Marcy handed out bottles of water. A short while later, I sat alone on the back bench, dressed in my wetsuit, holding on to the chainmail. I prayed over the chained links the way a knight might have a thousand years prior before going off on a crusade.

"You okay, Brandon?"

I didn't want to show fear in front of Marcy, as she needed a good role model for the Christian faith. Then I remembered two things. Marcy had a good radar, and I wasn't Jesus. "I gotta be honest, kiddo. I'm praying for a safe dive, and please don't give me jabs about my faith."

"I promise," she said. "I don't envy what you're about to do."

"I have a feeling the underwater frenzy I ran into on

the last dive is going to be a rerun. A rerun I don't care to watch."

"What can I do?"

I handed her the emergency first aid kit Drake had sent down. It was a supercharged version of the one I carried in my go bag. "There's a tourniquet and quick clot in there in case I come up fast with a wound. Bleeding out is the main danger. We're easily an hour away from the nearest ambulance."

Her hands shook as she took the first aid kit from me. "Okay."

"I hate to say it, but that chainmail ain't gonna help if a big one bites down," Luke said. "He'll crunch your bones into dust."

"Gee, thanks for the pep talk."

"I got your back, though," Luke said, lifting an ancient Winchester lever-action rifle. The wood stock was worn and the barrel blued.

"That thing still work?"

"Course she does."

"The old girl is chambered in 44-40, Lucas McCain's caliber. She'll do the job if anything is anywhere near the surface."

"Unfortunately, I'll be twenty feet down," I said, starting to put on the chainmail.

ELEVEN

Once in the chainmail, I put on a headlamp, put the wrench and pry bar to the belt, and strapped the dive knife to my leg along with the ankle bracelet. I tucked the speargun under my arm and held the shark stick in front while I eased into the water rather than drop in backward. It was important to make the least noticeable surface splash possible. Any sudden movement could mimic a fish in distress and would attract sharks. With no fins circling me, I gave a quick thumbs-up and let air out of my BCD. The water temp was warm, and visibility was slightly better than the day before coming in around ten feet. My heart pounded like never before. The only other time in my life I can remember it going this fast was the first time I kissed Annie. It seemed like the emotional extremes of falling in love and fearing death were my two heart-racing triggers. I much preferred the former.

At twenty feet, I touched the sandy bottom. Something moved under my fin. I lifted my right leg, and a large crab hung onto the end of the fin. A few strokes and the little fella dropped away to the sandy bottom. I switched the headlamp to high intensity and still could not see more than a few feet in front of me with the sediment stirred up from my fin. I found the anchor line and worked myself into concentric circles outward from it. In less than a minute, I found a half-empty chum bag of fish heads floating nearby. I turned around, looking for the sign of sharks but saw nothing. The chum bag was tethered to another cement slab where an identical suitcase was wired, and weighted. It was then I noticed this location didn't have a blinking electronic device like the last drop point. I took out my knife and cut the chum bag free removing any further incentives for predators. The pry bar made short work of the bolt holding the suitcase. I removed the weighted belt from around the suitcase and soon floated upward with the package in tow. When I broke the surface, Luke had his rifle aimed at me.

"I'm fine," I said. "You can put that down and help me with this."

* * *

MINUTES LATER, I was out of the chainmail and had my wetsuit peeled off to my waist. I sat on the stern bench, just soaked up the warm sun, and praised God for a safe dive.

Luke started up the boat, and we continued north toward the final drop point. "Let's hope the next dive is as uneventful."

Marcy looked at my tank. "How much air you have left?"

"About ten minutes," I said, kneeling to pry open the suitcase. "So I gotta make the last dive quick."

"It was a miracle you didn't encounter that electronic gizmo and sharks this time," Luke said.

"No, it wasn't," Marcy said, scanning something on her cell phone.

"Why'd you say that?"

"Remember those bad storms we had recently?"

"I remember," I said, popping the cover open. I placed the first bag of heroin into a duffle bag. "Hand me that small cinderblock and zip tie, will you."

"I think the storm moved the device off this location and toward the shore. Here, look at this." She showed me a map of the lower Chesapeake Bay. This is where you just picked up the drugs, and this is where one of the shark attacks occurred." She pointed toward the shoreline. "It's almost directly across from this drop point, about ten yards from the shore. I bet if we went over there, we'd find the device."

I scratched my head. "So the storm washed the device toward the shore, which is why the attack occurred there?"

"Makes sense," Luke said.

"Not bad, Marcy," I said, struggling to keep up with the sixteen-year-old's fast-moving brain. "If that's the case, then if the other shark attack was a scuba diver near Tangier Island—which is where we're now heading —can you pull up a location of that attack and see how close it lines up with my next dive spot?"

"You're hoping that device was washed free as well?" Marcy asked, scrolling through her phone.

"It would be unbelievably good news."

After a few minutes, she said, "Uh, sorry, Brandon. That shark attack seemed to be right near the dive spot you need to go to. If I had to guess, the electronic device is still near the dive location."

My stomach turned into a knot. "So much for catching another break."

* * *

Clouds soon overshadowed the sun, and the waves picked up, slamming the little wooden boat up and down. By the time we reached the third dive spot, it was late afternoon, and a light rain had started to fall. In the distance were dark streaks across the sky, showing where the drizzle turned into heavy rain. I could have kicked myself for not checking the weather. Luke dropped the anchor but left the engine idling. While Luke topped off the fuel with a spare jerry can of gas, I dressed in the chainmail again and planned to carry both the speargun and shark stick again. I made sure the tourniquet was the first thing Marcy would grab if she had to open the first aid kit.

"Good luck," Marcy said.

"I don't believe in luck, Marcy."

"We believe in Providence," Luke added.

"Amen," I said before sliding over.

The headlamp did little to cut through the murkiness. With no sunlight, what visibility I had on the last dive was now gone. It felt like I had descended into a demonic lair, filled with creatures waiting to attack me. Were this a spiritual battle, the only weapons I had, according to Ephesians 6's Armor of God, were the Sword of the Spirit, or the Word of God, and to rebuke evil, you needed to speak. Ironically, I couldn't utter a word from the Bible to repel any attack due to the regulator stuck in my mouth.

This dive was deeper than the other two coming in around twenty-five feet, and my air was running dangerously low. I would have just enough time to find the suitcase, pry it free, and sprint to the surface. As I neared the sandy bottom, my right fin rubbed up against something big. I tried to stop the descent, but it was too late. The head of a five-foot bull shark swung around to face me. He was clearly annoyed at my presence. It swam off, flinging its tailfin in my direction in a clear, aggressive manner. I didn't know if it moved off from my shark-repellent anklet, or maybe I just scared it. Regardless, it took tremendous effort to keep my breathing slow and rhythmic. I reached the bottom and, within moments, found the flashing beacon of the electronic device. It had no *off* button, and I assumed its controls must be remote. The chum bag floated nearby with only one or two fish heads left in it.

This suitcase was smaller than the other two. It took a bit more effort to pry it free from the cement base. While I did this, two sharks circled a few feet above. I stopped what I was doing and used the speargun to poke the bigger one, a six-footer, in the lower jaw. The animal didn't swim off, instead it started movements that seemed frantic, like it was going to attack. I had only annoyed the creature. To my right, the blinking light of the electronic box suddenly shut off. A moment later, the sharks moved off and disappeared into the ether. I checked my air to find it on reserves. With the sharks gone, I refocused on the hasp. It popped, and the suitcase was free.

I held the suitcase in my left hand with the shark stick leashed on that same wrist and the speargun in my right hand. Not ten feet into the ascent, I realized why the electronic device had shut down. Two human shadows with flashlights descended in my direction. I shut off my headlamp and swam off to the right, but it was clear they noticed me. I dropped back down to the cement platform. Both men were armed with spearguns. They approached, and one leveled a speargun and took a shot. I was shocked at how fast the bolt went underwater. The barb ricocheted off the left thigh of my chainmail. It didn't penetrate, but it still hurt like a hundred bee stings. I held up the suitcase for them to see before letting it go, and swimming away.

After ten yards, I made the mistake of looking back. One of them had gone after the drugs. The other was in pursuit with a speargun in front of him. He was fast and gaining on me by the second. I inflated my BCD and started my ascent again. I turned around and lowered the speargun in warning. He clearly saw the weapon but didn't slow down. I could tell by his strokes he was enraged. With no alternatives, I pulled the trigger, but my bolt missed its mark. A moment later, a bolt from his speargun swished past my regulator. I continued my ascent, but a few strokes later, he had grabbed onto my right fin. I wiggled free of the fin, but he latched onto my leg. Beneath him, I could see the faint light of his partner starting his ascent. I had only a handful of breaths of air left and couldn't free myself from his grasp. His muscular build and bearded face revealed the man I had met in the yard of Cape Charles Customs. I wondered if he recognized me as well. I remembered the conversation with Cassie, who said his name was Charlie. He was the boss of the yard and, according to her, was as mean as a snake.

A moment later, the man known as Charlie lived up to his reputation. A shiny dive knife appeared in his hand, and he slashed at my legs. The chainmail deflected the strikes and seemed to infuriate Charlie further. I kicked him in the head with my finless boot, but he held on to my leg like a pit bull unwilling to give up a meaty bone. I was out of air, and out of options. I had no choice but to rip the shark stick from my wrist and slam it into his bicep. It exploded with a pop, followed by a cloud of red blood and tissue. Charlie let go and frantically thrashed about. Even with the regulator in his mouth, I could hear him scream in pain. While he did this, I grabbed his backup octopus regulator and took a long drag. That shotgun shell of the shark bangstick was powerful enough to kill a five-hundred-pound shark and might do the same to Charlie if he didn't get medical attention soon.

I took a final breath from his regulator just as his dive buddy reached us with the suitcase. I couldn't tell if he had taken the time to reload his speargun, but I fought the urge to flee to the surface and stayed to address the new threat. I used the thrashing of Charlie's distraction to rip the second diver's mask off. With both men disabled in different ways, I restarted my ascent, but was hit in the side by something big. I turned to see the dorsal fin of a massive bull shark swim by. It must have been eleven feet long. With a single swish of its tale, it tore off down toward Charlie's bleeding arm. I watched in horror as it bit into his torso and dragged him down into the depths, his headlamp the only thing leaving a trail of light. Charlie's dive buddy started his ascent but was hit from behind by another shark. He dropped the suitcase and fought against the beast with his dive knife. I turned away from the horrific scene I'd carry with me for the rest of my life and focused on reaching the surface.

I had no idea what I would encounter once I broke the surface. The divers came from a second boat that could have armed men on board, so I chose to surface about twenty yards south of Luke's boat. A fast boat was tied to Luke's boat with a man holding a bolt-action rifle. I couldn't see Marcy or Luke. The sky was pitch dark, and the rain had picked up along with the waves. I reloaded the speargun with the one spare bolt I had brought. The shark stick was useless and had to be reloaded on the boat, so I let it go.

I removed my empty tank and let it float away. After several deep breaths, I ducked back underwater and swam toward the boats. It would be a long sprint, but I had to get to the blind side of Luke's boat. By the time I reached the underside of the fast boat, my lungs were on fire. I pushed on, praying for strength to go another few yards. I popped up beneath the bow of Luke's boat. After a few deep breaths and assurance no one heard me, I used my dive knife to cut Luke's anchor line. The heavy waves moved his boat away from the other boat by a few yards which told me they weren't tied together. Lightning flashed overhead, adding to the severity of the situation. I leashed the speargun to my forearm, dropped my remaining fin, and did a pull-up over the bow of Luke's boat.

The man in the fast boat was a middle-aged bald man with a familiar face. It was the cop I saw from the kayak, Sergeant Cox. He was dressed in civilian attire and busy looking over the side for his scuba buddies. I dropped down into the deck of Luke's boat and slipped on something slick. It was a large pool of blood. Luke was facedown, unconscious with a gash on his head. Marcy was nowhere on board. I checked, and Luke had a pulse. I had to triage the situation before I could help him. The next flash of lightning, I stood up and raised the speargun. Cox saw me and swung the rifle from the water's surface, but I got off a shot first. A moment later, the bolt pierced his shoulder, and he dropped the rifle with a shout followed by swearing. He leaned into the throttle with his body to move the fast boat a short distance away.

"Marcy?" I called, searching the water around the boat.

There was a grunting sound that came from Luke's body.

"Hold on, Luke."

I found Luke's lever-action rifle under the rear bench seat. The other boat was still only fifteen yards away but moving away by the second. I chambered a round in the rifle, but something told me not to fire. Marcy could be on that boat. I scanned the water's surface one final time to look for her before grabbing the emergency first aid kit. After applying the quick clot on Luke's head, he started to come around. I dragged him to the bow and raised his legs on a buoy. By the time I snapped an ice pack, the blood had stopped flowing from the wound. I wrapped his head with an Israeli battle dressing to hold the ice pack in place and covered him with several towels to keep him warm. Off the bow, I grabbed my tank and BCD, which floated next to the boat. As I lifted it onto the boat, I saw the floating torso of a diver bob up and down in the waves. The upper half of the body was all that remained. His pale, bearded face was frozen with the look of both horror and pain. I vomited all over the deck of the boat, my bile mixing with Luke's blood like some horrific soup.

I gunned Luke's boat in the direction of the fleeing fast boat, but the old engine was no match for the newer vessel. Besides, the bilge pump sounded like it was going to die. As if to reinforce the point, the engine stalled. After restarting the engine, I had no other choice than to head home. On the way back, the storm increased as if to add an exclamation point to the cluster that had been this dive. What had I done getting involved in something this far over my head? I vomited again, this time, nothing came up. The rest of the ride back, I prayed for forgiveness for my mistakes, for guidance, and pleaded with God to keep Marcy alive.

* * *

FIFTEEN MINUTES from the boat dock Luke sat up. He mumbled that the fast boat snuck up on them as it was so dark out, and they were held at gunpoint. "They took the other load of drugs," he said. "I tried to fight back when they took Marcy, but one of the men hit me with the butt of a rifle and I must have blacked out."

I told him how I tried to go after the boat but they were too fast and I had no choice but to head home. Luke cried like he was in physical pain. I knew it wasn't for his wound, but from the trauma of his granddaughter being taken. The sorrow reminded me of the distraught wails that once came from me when I found out my infant son had died. This was different, though. Luke still had hope and I knew who had taken Marcy.

"Marcy's not dead yet," I said. "We gotta pray."

"What are we going to do?"

I picked up my cell phone and dialed Drake. It went to voicemail. I called back and got voicemail again. I kept calling and after the fifth attempt, I heard a crackling voice on the other end. "What's wrong?"

"I need help," I pleaded.

I explained the dives—how I worked my way north and the bad guys must have worked their way south. I gave Drake the location of the last dive.

"Roger, I got nothing left," I said. "I overestimated my abilities, and now I'm worried there's a young girl who might be—" I broke down and couldn't finish the sentence.

"Okay, this is the plan," he said without hesitating. "I'm heading back there, but I'm still over South America. I don't want you doing any more dives. I'll get a diver to try to retrieve that last suitcase if it's still in the area. I want you to get someplace safe and wait to hear from me."

"What about the girl? I can't—"

"If they have the girl, they'll know where her granddaddy lives. You can't go back there."

"Dangit," I said. "We left the first case of drugs in his barn."

"Just get somewhere safe and wait for me."

"How long?"

"Forty-eight to seventy-two hours max. Don't do anything rash, son."

* * *

By the time we reached the boat ramp, I had the chainmail off and my wetsuit stripped down to my waist. The deck of the boat was an absolute mess of gear, vomit, and blood. Thankfully, we were the only ones at the ramp due to the bad weather. I tied off the boat and helped Luke onto the dock and over to the truck. He all but collapsed into the passenger seat. It took me a half hour to load the boat back onto the trailer.

Once on the road, I looked over at Luke. He was ashen and barely conscious. "I should get you to a hospital."

"Just take me home, Brandon."

"No can do, my friend. Your house isn't safe. If MS-13 have Marcy, they'll soon know where you live. I'm gonna take you to Virginia Beach and—"

"No."

"Then give me an alternative?"

"Take me to my church in Eastville."

"Your church?"

"My pastor," Luke mumbled. "He's a patriot and part-time EMT. He'll know what to do. Go up and take this right."

TWELVE

I FOLLOWED LUKE'S DIRECTIONS, AND TWENTY MINUTES later, we drove down a quiet tree-lined side road to face an adorable little white church. The gravel parking lot was empty except for an older maroon Dodge minivan. Luke directed me around back, where a small parsonage was situated.

"A long time ago, this used to be Pastor Bob's house. We now use it for traveling missionaries and guests to stay in. We'll be able to rest here."

I shut the truck off. As I helped Luke out of the passenger seat, a mid-fifties balding man with a gray mustache came out of the back of the church. His smile faded when he saw Luke's bandaged head, and his walk increased to a run.

"What happened?"

"I'm assuming you're Pastor Bob?"

"Yeah. What happened to Luke?"

"Just get me into the parsonage," Luke said. "Brandon will explain."

Pastor Bob pulled out a ring of keys and handed them

to me. "The blue key opens the parsonage. I'm gonna get my first aid kit in my van and will meet you in a minute."

I walked Luke up the few steps to the front door of the small ranch home and fumbled with the keys. In moments, Pastor Bob was at my side and took the keys from me to open the door. He took Luke's free arm and slung it over his shoulder. Together, we walked Luke through a sparse living room into one of two bedrooms, where he collapsed onto an antique twin bed covered in quilts.

"What happened?" Bob asked.

"He was attacked while we were out on his boat," I said. "Guy pulled up in another boat and clubbed him. I was scuba diving at the time. Luke's lost a lot of blood from that head wound."

Bob lifted the bandage and ice pack to look at the gash on Luke's head. He then took out a penlight and shined it in Luke's eyes. Luke swatted his hand away. "Sorry, my friend, but I need to see if you have a concussion, or worse?"

While Bob checked on Luke, I went back out to the boat and loaded all my gear into two duffel bags and brought them into the house. After changing back into shorts and a shirt, I checked back in on Luke.

"Brandon," Luke's voice was a whisper, and he motioned me closer with his hand. "You can tell Bob everything."

Bob used rubbing alcohol and a towel to wipe the dried blood from Luke's head wound. "What has my old friend gotten himself into?"

For the next few minutes, I explained an abbreviated story to Bob. I left out a lot of details but hit enough of the high notes to give him a ten-thousand-foot view before finishing with Marcy's abduction. Luke added that no local authorities could be trusted, including the Coast Guard, and that a local cop was the pilot of the other boat.

"You fellas are in a real spot," Bob said. "Normally, I'd insist Luke go in for X-rays, but it sounds like people might be looking for him. Hand me that razor, Brandon." I handed him a disposable plastic razor, and Bob proceeded to shave a portion of Luke's thin gray hair away around the gash on the top of his head. He cleaned and disinfected the area, used a couple of zip stitches to close the wound, and covered the bulbous lump with a gauze pad and a new ice pack.

"I need to leave Luke here," I said.

"What are you going to do?" Bob asked, continuing to check Luke over.

"I'm waiting on a friend from government to show up, but I want to drive by Luke's place to see if it's been raided."

"Here," Bob said, handing me his key ring. "Take my car. Everyone in Cape Charles knows Luke's truck."

* * *

I IGNORED Roger Drake's advice and, twenty minutes later, drove past Luke's property. Pastor Bob's car was a perfect old inconspicuous minivan with a bit of rust and peeling clear coat. It was the perfect gray-man vehicle to drive around in. No one was on Luke's property that I could see from the street. The traffic on Route 13 was busy, but it was a highway. I drove down the street, parked at a gas station, and walked through the woods to the back of Luke's property. I had my Smith and Wesson along with two spare mags in case anyone showed up. At the back of Luke's barn, I waited for ten minutes with no sign of activity. The drugs were still hidden in the back of his biplane where we had left them. I loaded them, along with the few of my items left in the guesthouse, into my rental car and drove it over to the gas station. I transferred everything to Pastor Bob's van and headed back to the parsonage. At least if anyone showed up at the property, there would be no trace of me or the drugs.

* * *

BACK AT THE PARSONAGE, I told Bob what I had done. "Wherever that boat was going with Marcy was farther than our destination, so they haven't had time to process, or break the girl yet. It won't be hard to figure out whose daughter she is and discover her grandfather's address. I bet by morning, the farm will be ransacked."

"The drugs are?"

"In your minivan," I said. "Congrats, Pastor Bob, you're street value just skyrocketed."

He gave a half grin and thumbed toward the room Luke was in. "Looks like our friend is going to be okay. No sign of fracture or even concussion that I can tell. He should be taken to a hospital, but based on extenuating circumstances, I'll monitor him from here for the next twenty-four hours. Luke mentioned you're a PI and do some side work for the government."

I nodded. "I'll get the drugs out of here as soon as possible. As soon as my friend—"

A text interrupted us. It was Drake. The text read: *Stuck in Mexico. Weather-hurricane. Locked down. ETA unknown...*

My stomach tightened. "Excuse me for a moment, Bob." I was on my own, and Marcy was in danger.

I walked outside and started praying and thinking.

The church property seemed to be designed for such things. Behind the parsonage was a mature forest with a trail that meandered through a canopy of trees. The dense pathway allowed just enough light through to make it feel like it was otherworldly. I was up against MS-13, an entity with more manpower and resources than the Canadian government. My only options were to wait for Drake to show up and hand everything off to him or reach out to some other random contact in government he might know.

Annie texted a simple message that read: *Thinking about you. Please be safe.*

I wanted to call and tell her about the diving incident, the shark attacks, and the men dying. About Luke's injury and Marcy's abduction, but I knew she'd be crippled with panic and would never sleep. Annie needed to be on her A game for the girls. Still, the images flashed before my eyes of the two men dying in one of the most horrific ways possible. The sad irony was their eternal destination was going to be far worse than how they met their fate. I responded to Annie's text asking her to keep us all in prayer.

Annie texted right back: *Trust in the Lord with all thine heart; and lean not unto thine own understanding. In all thy ways acknowledge Him, and he shall direct thy paths. Proverbs 3:5-6.*

I'm glad I hadn't told her about the day's events, or else she might have sent me something different. Instead, she sent me exactly what I needed.

I prayed out loud. "Father, what would you have me do? We need to get Marcy back. She doesn't know you yet."

I wasn't expecting an audible response but hoped something would come to me. An epiphany maybe? I continued through a winding path of mature maple trees and reminded myself that God was in control, even during this chaos. The pathway, just like the Bible passage mentioned, straightened out, and so did my thoughts.

Could I use the drugs in exchange for Marcy?

I'd need help. Immediately, the image of my tech friend, JT, came to mind. He was a Massachusetts transplant who fled to South Boston, Virginia, from a failed marriage and failed multi-million-dollar software venture. As with many things, time helped heal old wounds. God finished healing his broken heart when he came to faith. Things seemed to be going well for him as of late. JT returned to the world of computers, technology, and software development. Recently, he purchased an abandoned building that had once been a hospital in the early 1900s and turned it into his new software headquarters.

I video-dialed JT, who picked up on the first ring. He had on a suit jacket and a dress shirt with a Boston Red Sox ball cap. For some reason, the style worked for him. "What's up, brotha?" he said in a flagrant Massachusetts accent.

"How's it going?"

"Hold on a sec," JT said. "Someone wants to say hello."

A moment later, an adorable blond-haired girl stuck her face in front of the video chat. "Brooke, how are you doing?"

"I'm good," the young girl said. "When is Emily coming back from the beach? Mom said I could invite her over to play?"

"She should be home. I'm staying an extra day or two for work."

"Thanks, Mr. Hall." She handed the phone back to JT and ran off.

Once I thought Brooke was out of range, I whispered, "She looks well?"

"She may never be the same," JT said, "but she's alive, and healing more each day. All thanks to you."

"That was all God," I said, referring to her rescue from child traffickers in the Dismal Swamp.

"You look stressed, dude?"

"I'm kind of in a pickle—"

"You?" JT laughed. "How could you possibly get into a pickle?"

I heard a female's voice from the back of the office. "If that man asks you for a kidney, you give it to him, Jason."

JT did a mock salute to the woman offscreen. "Yes, ma'am."

A moment later, Brooke's mom, Sally, walked into view behind JT. "You doing okay, Brandon?"

"I'm okay," I said. "I got recruited to work on a case while on vacation, and I need your husband's wicked-smaaht tech brain."

"That's a horrible Boston accent," JT said. He turned to Sally. "Sweetie, can you tell Becca to hold my calls?" A moment later, Sally was gone from the screen, and I heard a door close. "Okay, talk to me."

I didn't hold back. I trusted JT and told him everything. From what started as simply looking into Marcy's extracurricular friendships, to her mom's job running drugs, and the information we recovered for the drop locations for the drugs. I told of Cassie's murder, the shark encounters, and the two men's horrific underwater deaths. Finally, I ended with Marcy's abduction. JT listened and only responded with a few whistles as if he couldn't believe the fantastic stories he heard.

Finally, he said, "Sounds like you stumbled into a James Bond movie, brotha. What can I do?"

"I'm not sure yet. I recognized the person who took Marcy. He's a cop on the take."

"Name?" JT asked, typing away in the background.

"Cox. No idea of the first name. He's a sergeant. Lives in a mansion on the beach in Cape Charles. Easily above his pay grade."

"Stanley Cox," JT said, continuing to type. "He's put in for PTO this week."

"How do you—"

"Daddy's good at what he does." JT always called himself Daddy and spoke in the third person when he was in his computer zone.

"I'm gonna drive by his house as well as Cape Charles Customs to check things out," I said, "but I think it's highly unlikely Cox would bring Marcy back to either of those places. I'm guessing he's partnered with some other people and has her in a place up the coast somewhere."

"What should I do?"

"Not sure," I said. "If this goes the way I think, then I'll need to make contact with MS-13. I need to find a way to keep Marcy alive until my friends in government make it back here to take this off my plate or get her myself if time runs short via a swap for the drugs."

I could hear typing in the background. "Okay, I'm gonna start with Cape Charles Customs's computers. When I hack into their computers, I may be able to find something out."

"Like?"

"An offsite facility. Someplace they could be holding the girl."

"Other ideas?"

"I can make contact with MS-13 via the dark web and try to broker a deal once I hear back from you."

"How would you do that?"

"Daddy has his ways."

* * *

I SPENT the next half-hour in the bathroom of the parsonage. First, trimming my beard with a pair of scissors I found in the cabinet. Once it was short enough, I shaved the rest of it down to nothing. More wrinkles had appeared on my skin that weren't there before. Worry lines, as Annie would call them. I went into the shower and rinsed off. It always felt good to take a hot shower and get into a clean pair of jeans, a button-down, and my broken-in cowboy boots. Like Batman's cape and cowl, this was my go-to work outfit. I found a Red Sox cap JT had given me that I kept in my go bag and wore a pair of sunglasses. Coupled with Pastor Bob's minivan, I would be both unrecognizable and untraceable.

Upon exiting the bathroom, Pastor Bob was taken aback when he saw me. "Sorry to startle you," I said. "I do this from time to time when blending in is imperative."

"Makes sense."

"May I use your van again?"

"Be my guest," he said. "Our patient is resting, so I'd just shut the front door quietly on your way out."

"Roger that, and thank you for everything."

* * *

I SPENT the next hour driving around Cape Charles. From what I could see from the road, Sergeant Cox's house was empty. No cars were in the driveway. I parked in the lot behind the Veterans War Memorial again and gazed across the water at Cape Charles Customs via the monocular from my go bag. From what I could see, it was empty as well, with zero cars in the lot. It was as if someone told them what happened at sea, and there was a good chance the Feds were gonna soon raid the place. It would not have surprised me to see a tumbleweed pass by.

Before heading back to the parsonage, I tried one last long shot. I pulled up to the strip mall down the street from Luke's farm and decided to drive around back. As soon as I made the corner behind the grocery store, I could see the pickup trucks in the distance near the overgrown baseball field. I parked the minivan a distance away but left it running. The last time I had been there, I had my butt handed to me, but at least Marcy came home with me.

The same pickup trucks were there with the same group of kids hanging out. It looked like they had started to pack up for the day. One of the girls was in the process of picking up fast-food wrappers that had blown from the tailgate of one of the pickup beds. Ironic, they looked out for the environment but sold drugs. I guessed no one had given them the news that their supplier was in distress. Everyone on the back of the pickups turned when they saw the figure get out of the minivan. I continued to walk toward the group and the music cut. No one seemed to recognize me without the beard. Instead of beachwear, I had on my cowboy boots, jeans, and a button-down. A couple of kids walked up to me as if to block my way, but I brushed past them, giving each a hard shoulder. Finally, a male about my height stepped up to block the path. He was about to say something I assumed was gonna be snarky, but I kicked him in the groin, which took the wind out of his proverbial sails.

The one I was looking for jumped up. The leader, Jeremy, was in a tank top, baggy shorts, and flip-flops. He had been making out with a girl and had a bottle of some hard liquor in his hand. I rushed past a few knuckleheads before they could even cock their fists. An early twenties skinny male got in my path. One punch to the side of his head knocked him out cold. By this time, Jeremy had dropped both the bottle and girl, and was in a crouched position prepping for a fight. Had I time to go one-on-one, I would have welcomed the challenge. Instead, I had my Smith and Wesson out and pressed against his forehead before he could cock his fist.

"Tell your buddies to back away," I said.

"You are a Fed," he said, recognizing me.

"Tell 'em!"

"Back off, guys!"

The group backed away.

"I knew you were law enforcement," Jeremy said. "I'll walk."

"Why, because I carry?" I laughed. "How about I'm a red-blooded Virginian who exercises his second amendment rights." I grabbed Jeremy by his greasy hair and walked him through the crowd with my nine-millimeter to the side of his head. "What product do you use in your hair, dude? It feels like a Philly cheesesteak."

"Shut up!"

"Girls must love all hundred and ten pounds of you with that wannabe gangsta attitude," I laughed.

"You come back here, and it will be the last thing you do," he said, trying to sound tough.

"Trust me," I said, stopping about ten feet outside of the group. "You haven't made me feel welcome." I turned back to face everyone. "Listen up. Your supplier has skipped town."

"Don't know what you're talking 'bout, guy," one of the males said.

"Your drug supplier!" I shouted. "You know, MS-13? They went bye-bye, and their onshore contact at Cape Charles Customs asked me to say *vaya con dios* as well. Go ahead and try to reach them."

A couple of the kids looked toward Jeremy who winced like I spilled the proverbial beans. This told me Jeremy was the only one who had contact with their onshore supplier. It must have been a bottleneck organization, with him being the channel through which information flowed. The rest of the kids probably set up drug drop-off locations at Jeremy's beck and call.

"You're wasting your time, bruh," Jeremy spat.

"Then let's get out of here, bruh." I mocked him loud enough for everyone to hear again. Before leaving, I said, "A little word of advice. This place is going to be swarming with Feds soon. Whatever protection local corrupt law enforcement offered you guys is evaporating. I suggest you go home to Mommy and Daddy and tell them to lawyer up. Far more important, get right with God. Your lives are about to get very complicated." I turned to the girls standing back by the pickup trucks. "Girls, even if you were just hanging out here to party, expect your lives to get very serious very soon. All of you go home. Now come along, young Jeremy."

THIRTEEN

I HALF DRAGGED JEREMY TOWARD THE MINIVAN. THE farther we moved from the group, the more I could see his shoulders slump. It was as if he was losing connection to his power source. I zip-cuffed him and tossed him in the passenger seat. Inside, I put my gun away in the appendix holster and wiped my hand on his tank top. "Dude, you put way too much crap in your hair."

Once we started moving, he spoke in a whiny, passive tone. "Seriously, you a Fed?"

"I told you I'm a Virginian. I'm not even LEO, but my spec ops buddies are on their way here from the government and are bringing a world of pain with them."

"Okay, okay. Chill, dude."

"Now, there was a girl who used to hang with you guys named Marcy."

"Yeah, cutie. She was smart too. Fixed my cell phone."

"She's been kidnapped by someone working with MS-13, and I need to know where they might take her."

"How should I know?"

"Who's your contact here?"

"Why should I tell you?"

"Because that girl I just saw you make out with is gonna be the last female kiss you get for a few decades unless you work with me." He didn't say anything, so I added, "Don't drop the soap when you go away to the clink, bruh."

After a long pause, Jeremy said, "The cop. Cox. He's my contact."

"Where do you guys meet up?"

"Usually out on paddleboards in shorts. He's paranoid and makes sure I have no tech on me when we talk."

"He's the one who took off with Marcy," I said. "Where would he take her besides his house? Is there a place up the coast? A drop point? A place he meets up with other people from Cape Charles Customs?"

"No. I—"

"Jeremy, your future depends on this."

"I know Cox has a gambling problem, and whenever his wife kicks him out, he goes to his bookie's place."

"Where is it?"

"On the coast, about an hour north. I've been there once with him."

"Is it accessible by boat?"

"Yeah. Guy has a long dock going into the bay."

"Address?"

"I don't remember?"

"When was the last time you were there?"

"I've only been there once."

"When?"

"I can't remember," he said. "Maybe eight months ago?"

"Cell phone?"

"What?"

"Where's your cell phone?"

"My back pocket?"

I pulled the minivan over and pushed Jeremy aside so I could pull the cell out of his baggy shorts. "Hey, man. That's illegal search and seizure."

"Doesn't apply," I said. "I told you I'm not a cop. Now, what's your cell code?"

"Up yours."

"Anything happens to Marcy, I ain't going to bat for you."

"Who says you're going to bat for me anyway?"

I shrugged my shoulders. "Forget me for a second. It's my contacts in government who you need to go to bat for you. They'll act on my recommendations. If MS-13 thinks you even whispered their name, they'll hunt you down and slit your throat. You're gonna need to talk to me and my friends. You need a paradigm shift, my friend. Need to give up everything you have, and then, if you don't go to prison for life, maybe you'll get some leniency."

"I want a lawyer."

"You go right ahead and do that while I post on the dark web that I have you in custody, and you've already name-dropped Cape Charles Customs, Sergeant Cox, and linked them to MS-13. My guess is you'll be dead by tomorrow night."

"You can't do that."

"I can do anything I want. Now, what's your cell code."

He huffed. "54322."

I punched in the code and the cell phone unlocked. I dialed JT's number on my cell phone. He picked up, and I blurted out. "I'm calling you on another phone number you won't recognize. Make sure you pick up." I called him a moment later from Jeremy's phone and hung up my phone. "Can you work up a geolocation history on this phone?"

"Daddy can do anything."

I turned to Jeremy. "Where was the town where the bookie lived?"

"Exmore."

"I'm gonna text you a link," JT said. "Click on it, and it will allow me to hack the phone."

A moment later, the link appeared. I clicked on it, and my friend did his work. Five minutes later, JT gave me only one address in Exmore. I thanked him profusely and tore off north. Fifteen minutes into the drive, I took out my pocketknife and flipped it open. When I pointed it at Jeremy, he looked terrified.

"Turn," I said. He caught on and revealed his backside so I could cut the zip cuffs. "Don't make me regret doing that."

"Why are you taking me along with you?" he said, rubbing his wrists.

"You said this place was a mansion? I may need you to help me navigate the property."

"You mean like a backup?"

"Sure, Jeremy."

"Then give me a gun?"

"I may have been born at night, but I wasn't born last night," I said.

* * *

FOR THE REST of the ride, Jeremy kept asking for his phone back, and once or twice tried to puff up a bit, but I told him to shut up, reminding him how dark and lonely prison was. An hour later, I pulled up to a wrought iron gate. There appeared to be a video camera system on one of the two brick pillars, so I kept driving by. The brick wall perimeter tapered down to a hedge of finely trimmed shrubs which continued to act as a fence along the road. I drove until I found a place I could pull off and park the minivan out of site. It was along a tidal river which, from the tire marks, appeared to be a spot others had stopped at in the past for fishing, swimming, or other nocturnal activities. It was pitch dark out and the right time for spelunking. I popped the trunk and took out the chest rig. I would have left the helmet, but I needed the night vision, so I brought it along. I slung the AR-10 over my shoulder in a single-point harness.

"Dude, what the F—"

"Quiet," I said.

"I thought you said you weren't law enforcement?"

"I'm not," I said. "Let's go."

"You're not gonna give me anything?"

"No."

"What if you get shot?"

"Then you're on your own."

We got out and moved back along the road. Jeremy tripped over every twig, rock, and root he could find in his flip-flops.

"Can you keep it down?" I said. "We're getting near the home."

"My bad, dawg," he said. "I've only been here once. I didn't realize this property was so big."

We jumped onto the estate property at a break in the shrubs. It was a finely manicured place of about five acres of mostly lawn. A turn-of-the-century brick mansion sat on a small knoll that tapered down to the water. Only one or two lights were on in the house. There were no watchdogs or anyone else on the property that I could see. I approached the back of the home and found a couple of classic sports cars along with two new luxury SUVs in the driveway. There were supplies out near an eight-car garage telling me the vehicles had been detailed earlier.

"Stay here," I whispered, walking around to the open garage door.

"What if—"

"Stay out of sight."

Inside, I found an interior door that was locked but easy enough to jimmy with a credit card. I flipped up the night vision and stepped inside. With the helmet pushed down low and the rifle in the high-ready position, it would keep my face blocked from internal video cameras. The narrow hallway led to a dimly lit man-cave-type library. There were bookshelves filled with more DVDs than books. Dark wood cabinets lined the bottom of the space covered with decanters, bottles of wine, and a walk-in humidor took up the rest of the space. The room stunk of recent cigar smoke.

The rest of the house was barely lit and had no sounds, but I knew someone was home. Finally, I picked up the sounds of human noises. It was a conversation that came from the far end of the home on the same floor. I did everything to keep my breathing calm as I walked down the hallway. The hardwood gave way to white carpet, which would muffle any sound my boots made. On either side was a kitchen, then bedrooms and half bathrooms, a coat closet, front entrance. Finally, I approached the direction the conversation came from. It sounded the way I imagined a bookie would talk. Swearing interspersed with a few coherent sentences.

One person groveled back to another with an "I'm sorry."

I recognized the voice from somewhere, but I

couldn't place who or where. Was it someone I knew? I realized the voice was coming from a television. I burst into the room, the rifle leveled. A mafia movie played on a massive flatscreen in this master bedroom with a familiar actor waving a gun at another groveling actor. Across the room, in a canopy bed, was the fattest bald man I had ever seen. He was dressed in silk pajamas and lay flat on his back with a single bullet through his forehead. A look of fear permanently etched across his face. I scanned the rest of the room as well as the master bathroom, walk-in closet, and even under the bed but didn't find anyone else. Another desk in the corner of the room had a chair tipped over. Fat man must have been forced from there to the bed before he was questioned and dispatched execution style. There was a glass-paned door that exited into the back lawn. It was opened a crack.

Before leaving, I rushed through the second floor of the home just to make sure there was nothing else I missed. Upstairs I only found empty guest rooms and a young child's room. I assumed the fat man had shared custody of a child from a previous relationship. Back in the master bedroom, I exited the glass door, noting it was bulletproof, as were the other windows in the master bedroom. Just before I dropped the night vision back down, I picked up on a sliver of metal shining at the bottom of the steps. It was a pocket knife. Marcy's pocketknife she used to sharpen pencils. I picked it up and noticed the blade was broken off. She must have tried to use it to cut some sort of bonds or used it to try to escape. Once busted, she then dropped the useless tool as a sign.

I picked up the pace down the perfectly manicured lawn toward the water. Next to a boathouse, I found the body of Sergeant Cox with a bullet in the back of his head. My heart raced, terrified of what body I might find next. I rushed around the boathouse, looking for any sign of Marcy. The door was locked. Through the window, all I could see were kayaks and other water toys that hadn't seemed touched in months.

I tried to piece together what had happened. Cox must have fled by boat up the Chesapeake to his buddy's house, where he called for backup from other contacts within Cape Charles Customs. They, in turn, called someone within MS-13 who evaluated the situation from a strictly business point of view. With Cape Charles Customs out of commission, MS-13 decided to wipe everything. Another option was Cox needed medical attention from the wound he sustained on the boat from my speargun, and they didn't want him going to any doctor or hospital who would ask questions. The rumble of a boat engine snapped me out of the mind game. I sprinted toward the water.

I reached the beginning of a long, gorgeous dock that stretched for fifty yards out into the bay. At the end was the boat Cox had driven off in our last encounter. Another fast boat was pulling away from the dock. All I could make out was the driver was a male. I ran parallel to the boat along the beach on the lawn where I could pick up the most speed. The boat had to go slow as it was in a no-wake zone with rocks strewn about.

I dropped down on my stomach and flipped down a small tripod on the end of the AR-10. The rifle had a scope on it, which I flipped up. I never had an opportunity to sight in the rifle and hoped it was true. For one brief moment, my subconscious pinged. What if this man was a random stranger who was driving a boat, and I was about to shoot him? What if he wasn't MS-13? I scanned back to look for an outboard engine to target instead of the human target just to be safe. The boat had what looked like quad 150 horsepower engines. I'd have to take out four of them, which meant multiple rounds in each outboard. Too risky. I had to take a shot at the driver before he got out of range, but the .308 round was unforgiving. I said a prayer, exhaled, and pulled the trigger. A moment later, the person slumped over the controls, and the boat slowed down. If Marcy wasn't on board and this guy wasn't part of MS-13, then my life was over. I stood up and started a slow trot parallel to the boat again, trying to close the gap.

Suddenly, a familiar young girl popped up from a cuddy cabin beneath the boat's controls. In the clear moonlight, I confirmed it was Marcy. The knot in my stomach unwound at the sight of her brunette hair. I reslung the AR-10 and broke into a sprint. I dumped the helmet and started to loosen up the chest rig. The boat was still moving off in a northern direction.

"Marcy!" She turned in the direction of my voice but clearly couldn't see me in the dark. "You need to jump!"

By the time I made it onto the beach, I was free of gear. I watched as Marcy stepped up onto the stern bench. By now, I was in the shallows, barely able to hold my breath. Just as she swung her arms back to dive, a hand came up and grabbed her shirt to pull her back out of sight. Someone else had been in the cuddy cabin with her.

Whoever it was used the body of the driver as cover, jammed the throttle forward, and the boat moved off. I scrambled to shoulder the AR. In seconds, I locked in and fired off another round, but it thudded harmlessly into the corpse of the already deceased driver. I fired off another round with the same results. I lined up and fired off a round at the engines. A plume of smoke bellowed from the piece of now useless metal, but the three other engines were more than enough to continue to push the boat forward. I continued to fire off selective rounds at the three remaining engines until the boat was out of range. The last thing I saw was the blurry figure of the deceased driver pushed overboard before the boat continued north, out of range.

"No!" I shouted over and over until my voice turned to weeping.

Just as despair filled my heart, I realized there was still Cox's boat. I collected my gear and rushed back to the dock. By the time I reached the end, Cox's boat was half-sunken. Someone had pulled the drain plug from the back and punched a few more holes into the hull. The dash was torn up, and there was at least eighteen inches of water inside the boat, with more water collecting in the cuddy cabin by the second. I jumped in and franticly searched for a key to start it up and possibly get the bilge pumps going but found nothing. The boat continued to sink, and I was forced to abandon ship and watch it descend into the depths of the bay.

Walking back through the property, Jeremy was nowhere in sight. I noticed one of the SUVs that had been left outside the garage was missing. He was now on his own, and I could no longer help him. I made my way back down the road to the minivan and tore off back toward the parsonage, completely defeated.

* * *

ARRIVING BACK at Cape Charles seemed like entering another dimension. The town seemed quiet and different. Like everyone knew what was going on? Maybe the corruption went deeper than a few cops and a few Coast Guardsmen? Maybe there were store owners involved? It was late, I reminded myself. I drove past the Coast Guard station, but unlike Cape Charles Customs and the rest of town, this place seemed to be on high alert, with more activity going on than what seemed to be normal. Boats were moving in and around the water, and there was a flurry of activity around the base. I didn't stop as I knew my picture would be taken by some sort of security camera. I wished the coffee shop were open and I could have a conversation with my friend Charles Coyne. I drove by what was left of Cassie and Marcy's home. At this point, it was just a cement slab covered with a massive pile of charred wood. The scent of smoke mixed with pollen and humidity to create an unbreathable stench.

"But where are you now, Cassie?" I asked no one in particular. "Your daughter needs you more than ever." I refocused my message on my Father in Heaven. "Lord, please don't take Marcy without knowing you. Please keep her safe."

I stopped at an ATM and took out the maximum allowable amount of cash possible. There was only one path in front of me. With Drake stuck out of the country, I was going to be forced to confront MS-13 on my own and barter for Marcy. I had to get prepared.

FOURTEEN

Back at the parsonage, I checked on Luke, who channel-surfed in the bedroom. Pastor Bob snored in the twin bed across from him. In the living room, I made a follow-up call to JT, who had been waiting for me in his office.

"I couldn't hack into any servers at Cape Charles Customs," he said. "Whatever firewall they have in place has been hardened to the point of Fort Knox. I can tell you one thing. It sure ain't no auto body shop, brotha."

"What else you got?"

"I've been doing some research. What kind of heroin you got?"

"I don't know?"

"There's Mexican brown powder. There's China white which is Southeast Asian. Then there's Colombian white? A lot is mixed with fentanyl now and—"

"I have no idea what you're even saying," I said.

"Never mind. I've been geeking out since you left me alone for the past few hours. We're talking MS-13 for sure?"

"Yeah."

"So then it's Columbian heroin brought in via the Dominican Republic and plane. Then offloaded to probably a fishing or charter boat where it must be dropped for scuba pick up in the Chesapeake Bay."

"Sounds plausible."

"Price is ambiguous as it depends on purity, source, volume, and destination. And the more people involved in the transaction, the higher the price, as everyone gets a commission. However, the more people involved prior to you picking it up lowers the value of what you have to MS-13."

"How so?"

"Because everyone it passes by gets some sort of payoff. This is why it's much cheaper to buy drugs in South America than in the US. It needs to get past border patrol, customs, etc. All that is risk, payoff, etc., which equates to money spent. This deducts from the value of what you have. So purity level is important."

I thought for a moment. "Let's assume that because of the level of difficulty to retrieve the drugs, that it's a pure source, and—"

"Cape Charles Customs is the place they dilute it."

"Exactly."

"That would make sense," JT said. "How much product do you think you still have?"

"I have, like, two large bags full of heroin. I think about a hundred and fifty pounds total."

JT typed some more. "When talking drugs, brotha, we use the metric system. So that's a conversion of two-point-two pounds to one kilo. So Daddy moves a decimal spot and—" There was a pause. "If our assumptions are true about the purity, then you're looking at a value of up to $3+ million. Could be lower if they introduced cutting agents into the drug already."

"My gosh."

"Let me put you on hold for a minute," JT said. "If I get disconnected, I'll call you right back."

"Sure thing." I sat on the front steps and checked emails while I waited.

It took less than five minutes for JT to come back onto the video chat. I'm gonna go on the dark web and start name-dropping Cape Charles Customs to see what demons come out of hiding. I'm confident a proxy from MS-13 will snatch the bait. Once I make contact with the bad guys, what do you want me to do?"

I thought for a moment. The way Marcy explained Jeremy's group's drug protocols behind the town grocery store trickled back to mind. "If you make contact, I think—"

"When I make contact," JT corrected me.

"When you make contact," I clarified, "we have to make it seem like this is a business transaction and Marcy isn't as important as she seems. Tell them I want $200,000 in cryptocurrency deposited to an untraceable account that you set up, and I'll give them the coordinates for the first drop where they can pick up their drugs. If they agree to that, then I'll deliver the second case of drugs in exchange for $100,000 in crypto and the girl. Make sure you use the word girl rather than Marcy's name. It needs to be as impersonal as possible."

"You got some brass ones, don't ya," JT said, typing away.

"I want them second-guessing everything. They must believe Marcy isn't as important as she is."

"This will be quick, so keep your phone on."

"Thanks," I said. "Be ready for a counteroffer. I hope

my government friends get here soon. My stomach's in knots over this young girl's safety."

"One thing I've learned about God's timing," JT said. "It might be slow, but it's always on time. Stay prayed up."

I was overjoyed that in just a few short years, JT's spiritual journey had brought him full circle. A happenstance meeting at a local coffee shop in downtown South Boston led to a friendship between us, which turned into weekly coffee. In these meetings, we'd talk about life and why, if God were real, He would let JT's wife leave him, and let his business fall apart. Some of the conversations were tough, and I watched a man in a spiritual death spiral slowly come back to life from God's breath. It was amazing that this same man now encouraged me to stay in prayer. God was good, and JT was right, God's timing was perfect.

* * *

BACK INSIDE THE PARSONAGE, Pastor Bob was making tea in the galley kitchen. "Cup of tea?"

I waived the offer away. "No, thank you. Don't you have family and—"

"My two kids are grown, and my wife's at her book club. Besides, this is what my job entails. Caring for the flock."

"Can I do anything?"

"Yeah, it's near midnight. There's a second bedroom with a nice queen-sized bed I need you to go test out for me. You look exhausted."

"I am," I said. "If it's okay with you, I'll crash on the couch." I felt safer sleeping near the entrance with my nine-millimeter under the pillow and my boots on the floor next to me.

"Fine by me," he said. "I'll be in the twin bed next to Luke most of the night, keeping an eye on him. There's a John Wayne marathon on I'm hoping will keep him occupied until I think it's okay for him to sleep."

I poked my head into the bedroom to check on Luke. "How are you holding up?"

A new ace bandage held an ice pack in place over his head. The old man turned to me and gave me a weak thumbs-up. "You shaved?"

"Trying to go incognito." I was tempted to tell him about seeing Marcy, but my news was more bad than good. Instead, I just said, "No sleeping yet."

"He's well aware," Bob said from the kitchen.

With nothing left to do, I sat down on the leather couch in the living room. The image of Marcy trying to dive off the boat was seared in my mind. Even in the darkness, I could almost see the torment of both hope and desperation battling on her face as she was about to jump overboard before that dream was dashed. We were inches from our goal, and now she could be dead, tortured, or who knows what else? I forced the events out of my mind. It was a miserable defeat on every level. In the military, you were trained to assess the situation and move on, not dwell on your losses, but I had no team, no one to talk to. I felt alone even though I knew I wasn't. The Lord promised neither to leave nor forsake me, and I quietly repeated this to myself.

As if Pastor Bob could read my mind, he spoke from the kitchen. "If the world hates you, we know that it hated Him first."

"John 15:18," I said. "I know we're not guaranteed an easy go of things. In fact, being followers of Christ guarantees trials, but I'm grasping for His peace and joy to hold onto. You know, love, joy, peace, long-suffering, gentleness, goodness, faith."

"The fruits of the spirit."

"Yes, sir."

"You've prayed?"

"Constantly."

"Then, do what you can and leave it in His hands," Bob said, "and get some rest. There's nothing else to do. We're walking in complete faith at this point."

I went through a checklist of items that needed to get done. Everything that I could think of was complete. There was no trace of my presence on Luke's property. My rental car was offsite. If I didn't need it by the next day, I'd call the rental company to come pick it up. The drugs were with me, along with all my gear. No one knew where we were. At some point, I'd go into the truck and boat and organize my scuba gear, but for the moment, I was on hallowed ground and felt a level of supernatural protection that allowed me to close my eyes for a few minutes.

* * *

WHEN I WOKE, there was a thin fleece blanket over me. Minutes had turned to hours. On the coffee table next to me was a bottle of water and a piece of fruit. Outside, the sky was dark, and a drizzle flecked the window. I wanted to just roll over and go back to bed. Instead, I looked at my cell phone and saw a text from JT from four o'clock in the morning. It read: *Made contact. Giving terms. Stay tuned.*

Inside Luke's bedroom, he was up in bed watching the John Wayne and John Ford classic Western, *The*

Searchers. It was a story about a man searching for a lone survivor of a family massacred by an Indian raid in the 1800s. The young girl was taken hostage, and her uncle is on an obsessed journey to find and rescue her. Probably the worst movie for Luke to watch. The old man turned and gave me a half smile.

"You think our ending will be different?"

"I'm no John Wayne," I said.

"Yet, we have the Lord on our side."

"If He is for us—"

"Who can be against us," Luke finished the passage from Romans 8:31.

"How are you feeling?"

"Other than a headache, I feel fine."

"How are you holding up otherwise?"

"I'm exhausted, and sick with worry about my granddaughter. Any news?"

I thought for a moment about the sighting on the fast boat again but decided against sharing. "My tech friend made contact with MS-13. He's trying to broker a deal for us to exchange the drugs for Marcy."

"I've read about this group," Luke said. "They'll never go for it. I should have been on alert when that boat showed up."

"Stop the self-pity, Luke. It's not helping. I want you to focus on getting better so I can keep my focus on finding your granddaughter."

"I'm fine. I'll do what Bob says." He started to tear up. "Brandon, I can't handle another death. I—"

"Don't go there. I have at least several million worth of MS-13's drugs. They aren't gonna hurt her just yet. They want this product back." I repeated JT's mantra about staying in prayer.

Bob came back with muffins, fruit, bagels, and coffee.

"Sometimes, when you feel helpless, you simply pray and break bread," Bob said, placing the items on the small kitchen table. "Let me say grace. Father, I thank you for this nourishment for our bodies. Please strengthen Brandon for what lies ahead. In Jesus's name, we pray."

As I munched on a piece of fruit, JT called back. "Good news. They want the drugs, and they don't know who you are yet. We need to act fast, though. The dark web isn't as secure as people think, and it's only a matter of time before they pull info from that girl and/or trace out every connection her grandfather has. Make sure you wipe every piece of your existence from their lives. Then think how you want to do this and get back to me with a time and place."

"Roger that." I went into Luke's bedroom to find him still awake. "Luke, please tell me Marcy does not know my last name?"

"I've already thought about that," he said. "I've never told her your last name. You paid me in cash for the house rental, and I don't keep receipts. I have my cell phone with me, and that's the only place I have your phone number."

I exhaled and mentally started to go through every interaction I had with Marcy, and I didn't recall revealing my last name or where I lived.

My next message was to my buddy Tollers. I told him the complete situation, and there was a slight chance this girl with the photographic memory might have seen the license plate on his RV and that if she were tortured, it might give that info up. I told him it was unlikely, but still a slim possibility, and to be on alert.

"I'll keep an eye open here," he said. "I'll take the next day or two off and stick around the property, and I'll make sure to park my sheriff's car out front."

"I'm sorry," I said.

"Never apologize for the evil that other people do, Brandon."

"I need another favor," I said. "Just in case I missed something and she figures out who I was, it's a sure thing MS-13 will find out my farm's location."

"I'll keep a patrol in your area for the next few days as well. It will be easy enough to do, seeing as though the local Dollar Five Store was recently robbed."

The Bible said to be as wise as serpents and innocent as doves. To think like the enemy, but never act like the enemy. If I were the enemy, I'd go after my family. Marcy knew very little about me. Regardless, MS-13 had the resources of a small nation and might eventually figure out who I was. I texted Dad to stay alert and patrol the property with a firearm and that I'd explain later. He texted me back ten minutes later with a picture of his flintlock and tomahawk. The man drove me nuts. Dad loved American history and was stuck in the 1700s and, for some reason, would not embrace modern firearms no matter how dire the situation was.

Next, I had to think of a good place to swap the drugs for Marcy. MS-13 was vicious and would only agree to an exchange if it offered them a way to take me out. They didn't want word getting out that someone bested them in any way, shape, or form. I needed a defensible position for the swap. Difficult for them to access, yet easy for me to retreat from. I didn't know the Eastern Shore as well as Halifax County. Oh, how I wished Roger Drake and my spec ops friends were with me. Johnny Homer and Jose Paronto were ex-Navy SEALs who could fight off an entire platoon. The thought of Navy SEALs and naval battles, in general, reminded me I was on the seashore in Cape Charles, and somehow my mind drifted from Navy SEALs to naval battles and ocean warfare. I checked the time. It was early, but I figured Dr. Scott was up already. She picked up on the first ring.

"Dr. Spock, Brandon Hall here. Am I bothering you?"

"No, I was just arriving in South Boston. What can I do for you?"

"Being a historian and archaeologist, I need to pick your brain. What do you know about the ghost ships of Virginia's Eastern Shore? The ones sunk at Kiptopeke State Park?"

"Quite a bit," she said. "I'm originally from Norfolk and wrote a paper on them in grad school. Those are World War II boats sunk just offshore of the state park beach. They were placed there intentionally to create a breakwater. The amazing thing is, the boats are all made of concrete."

"I heard that."

"Only twenty-four were ever built. Of those twenty-four, nine were sunk at the park."

"Tell me about their construction. How tough were they? Did they ever come under enemy fire?"

"That's a good question," she said. "They were built of layers of mesh wire and concrete and rebar as there was such a shortage of steel at the time. They were thick, heavy, and slow, and used primarily as transports. I'm not sure what they could withstand as far as open-sea battles go. None that I know of ever came under enemy fire. They were mostly deployed in the South Pacific with two involved with the invasion of Normandy."

"Interesting."

"Why the interest?"

"I got hired for a side job while on vacation down on the Eastern Shore, and I may have to do some scuba diving near them."

"You can boat, dive, and fish near them but can't go on them. Besides, they're probably death traps with exposed rusted rebar and broken cement."

"Thanks, Dr. Spock. This is very helpful."

"Be safe, Brandon."

I used an app to locate the lat-long of the ships and started putting together a plan.

FIFTEEN

I GAVE JT THE ROUGH OUTLINE OF WHAT I WAS THINKING and would let him know by midday the final details. I texted Annie to assure her things were moving along and I would be home as soon as possible. She sent me pics of Emily and Amber painting wood trim in Amber's apartment and said she missed me.

It was late morning by the time my gear was organized and packed neatly in the back of Luke's truck. Bob had left to go home for clean clothes. I had asked him not to share too much information with his wife, which he agreed to do short of lying. I checked in one last time on Luke, who was asleep. Back on the couch, I read the Bible app on my phone and prayed about what lay ahead. Bob reentered just as I finished writing a note for them.

"Off to somewhere?"

"I've made contact with the terrorist group who has Marcy. I'm going dark for a day or two. Tell Luke if I don't see him again, it's not because I didn't try and that my friends in government will be here soon." I handed him a small bag. "Here, take these."

"What's this?"

"My cell phone, wallet, keys, pistol, and anything else that can ID me."

"Pistol? Don't you need this?"

"That pistol has a serial number that can be traced to me. I have other weapons in the truck that can't."

"What's your plan?"

"I'm going to try to exchange the drugs for Marcy near the sunken ships off of Kiptopeke State Park. I need to take Luke's truck. Tell him—" I caught myself choking up. "Tell him if I don't see him again that I did everything I could."

Bob held out his hand. "Let's pray before you head out."

* * *

TEN MINUTES LATER, I had a warm cup of coffee and a cold slice of pizza in hand as I drove Luke's old pickup over to the mainland. The dreary morning had given way to a cloudy, humid day. I needed a lot of gear and a place to top off my scuba tank with air. I didn't want to go to the dive shop in Cape Charles as it was more than likely being surveilled. In Virginia Beach, I found a massive fishing, boating, and dive shop. I hit another ATM and withdrew the maximum amount allowed again. With our family vacation spending money along with the ATM runs, I figured I'd have enough for the purchases needed. I proceeded to pick up a small rubber raft and paddles along with a teen's mask, snorkel, flippers, and some old, weighted dive belts. The raft would be the primary escape plan, with the mask and fins as a backup retreat plan. Both of which involved Marcy coming back with me.

At a grocery store, I purchased four gallons of water along with beef jerky and PowerBars. I paid cash at a cell phone store for two prepaid phones in case I needed to make contact with anyone and destroy the phone thereafter. The first phone was a cheap older cell phone, but the second was a satellite phone that cost the same as a used car. It was hackproof and was guaranteed to work anywhere on the planet. Annie was going to lay an egg when she saw the receipts from all the purchases. My final stop was at an old-fashioned general mercantile store. It was one-half tourist store selling hoodies and candy, and one-half hardware store. I bought multiple lengths of thick chains and massive combination locks, along with a sleeping bag and two watertight plastic cases to house the drugs. Some last purchases included Mylar bags, ChapStick, and other toiletries to finish off a total purchase of what Annie will consider a small second mortgage.

AN HOUR LATER, I was back on the Eastern Shore. I found a sandy beach about a mile before Kiptopeke State Park and parked the truck. I texted Annie from the new satellite phone to check-in. She knew better than to ask about the new phone number as she had seen me use this tactic in past jobs. I changed into my wetsuit and launched the inflatable using Luke's old two-stroke motor I had stripped off his boat. It was too much engine for the dinghy, but the horsepower would get us out of there quickly if needed. Fortunately, it had started to rain again, forcing the few remaining boats in the area to flee. With all the gear, weapons, food, as well as the drugs, the small raft was overflowing and just remained above the waves.

It was late afternoon by the time I reached the outskirts of the half-sunken boats. The old husks were covered with moss, barnacles, and even seagrass. Time and weather had revealed fissures in the thick hulls which had a beam of about fifty feet.

I spent an hour skulking around the boats praying for the right spot to make my headquarters. I found a gap in the side of boat number eight and saw that it was both level and dry inside. I tied off the inflatable and unloaded most of the gear into the hull. This would be my observation post. The next step was to go back out in the dinghy and find two underwater spots to plant the drugs. I had on my wetsuit and debated whether or not to wear the chainmail over it, but I remembered the logic behind its purpose. There were no electronic devices or chum bags nearby. These two dive spots of my choosing would be shark-free. Still, I wore the electronic shark repellent around my ankle just in case.

I used dive belts as ballast around the watertight cases and planted the first load of drugs in the shallows in between the gap in boats four and five. The dive was easy. There were lots of fish around the sunken hulls of the boats. Had it been any other time, I would have enjoyed the shallow dive. The second stash I planted at the end of the southernmost tip of ship number nine, where it dropped off to twenty-five feet of water. In case MS-13 showed up with two boats, this large gap in dive locations would allow me to split the boats while still keeping an eye on both locations from my observation post in boat eight.

Just like Jeremy's drug trades, each transaction would be a two-tiered transaction. MS-13 would be given the location of the drugs first, but they would find the suitcase chained to exposed rebar from beneath the boats. Unless they wanted to waste time bringing an underwater torch to cut through the thick chain and lock, they would have to wait for me to give them the combination to the lock, which I'd do after the first crypto transaction was complete.

BACK ON BOARD BOAT EIGHT, I dragged the inflatable dinghy inside the hull via a large gap in the portside hull. The next step was to make contact. I texted JT and told him to reach out for the first deposit of crypto. Once it dropped, I'd give him the lat-long coordinates to relay along for the first stash. I knew they would push back on the deal, but it was a starting point.

He texted back, saying they will only trade the girl for both stashes of drugs. I couldn't show my hand. If they knew Marcy was all I cared about, they would realize they held all the cards and would move us both into positions where the outcome would leave us both dead. I lowered my price to $100,000 for the first load and $75,000 and Marcy for the second. We both had to prove ourselves. Their answer was: *Girl only, and you get to live. We will find you and your family. Take this, and you live.*

I prayed about how to respond. "Lord, show me how to proceed."

I called JT rather than texting him. "What do you think?"

"They mean business, brotha. They know white hats monitor the dark web, too, so we gotta act."

"White hats?"

"The good guys in government. There are still some floating around up in DC, you know. We gotta move."

"Tell them the drugs are in two separate locations that can't be repositioned at this point. Offer $100,000 for the first half and $50,000 and the girl for the second half. Tell them I'm a mercenary and have to make my bills too."

"Why the sticking point on money?"

"I can't let on this is all about Marcy," I said. "Otherwise, they'll exploit her or just kill her. Tell them the packages are already locked and preplaced underwater, and locations are non-negotiable at this point. Tell them the good news is we can do the trade-in as quick as a few hours, but they need to have divers ready. We need to convince them that I need the money for my services, and the girl is for a client who is also paying me. We need to make this as clinical and sterile as possible. If they think it's just about Marcy, then we've given them everything."

"On it," JT said.

After the call, I prayed out loud again. "Lord, please take over."

JT called back. "The rep for MS-13 came back with $75,000 for the first half, with $50,000 and the girl for the second half."

"Done," I said.

"I'm kind of shocked they are going for it," JT said.

"They're probably using their leftover staff from Cape Charles Customs to do the trade," I said. "At this point, they've mentally washed themselves of the Eastern Shore. These employees are dead to them. Anything they can salvage using these remnant employees, the better. I'd bet MS-13 is promising their lives in exchange for recovering this last batch of heroin. My guess is they are going to kill them when this is all through anyway. Just like they are probably planning to kill me and Marcy regardless of our deal."

"That would make sense." JT paused for a moment. "Man, I wouldn't want to be you right now."

"Dude!"

"Sorry," JT chuckled. "It's the Bostonian in me. I'm trying to add some levity here, brotha."

"More prayer, less levity, please," I half-laughed.

"What do you want me to do next?"

"Send them the coordinates for the first drop of drugs and tell them a deposit of half of the first crypto batch should arrive in that account you set up ASAP. When they get to the site, I'll have a secondary lock for them to get through in exchange for the next portion. They can test the drugs to confirm they are legit, and then we go through the same process for the second drop location. Only this time, it will be for Marcy and crypto."

Five minutes later, JT sent off the coordinates for the first dive location, and $37,500 worth of some random cryptocurrency was soon dropped into an offshore account he had set up specifically for crypto. I was now committed to the path in front of me and felt claustrophobic in the old World War II boat just a half mile from shore.

For some reason, the calm water between me and Kiptopeke Beach reminded me of the parable of the rich man and Lazarus in the Gospel of Luke. The story told how there was a great fixed gulf between those who were tormented in hell and those safe in eternity. I knew my eternal destination was set in stone based on God's promises. He was going to wipe away every tear, sorrow, and pain, and my eternity with Him would be filled with joy. However, as I gazed back over the open bay, I was reminded that my time on earth had no fixed gulf. No protection from physical pain or suffering. There could very well be moments of hell.

JT texted that he was going to continue to stay over in his office and monitor everything until the job was complete. I thanked him profusely and started to settle in for what could be a long day or two. This situation reminded me of snipers I had met in the service. Stories circulated of how they would wait *on-scope* sometimes for hours or even days. Thankfully, I didn't have to stare down a rifle scope for forty-eight hours, but I did have to wait for the enemy to show up. Regardless, it was imperative I was in position long before MS-13 arrived. No matter what happened, I was going to be at a numerical disadvantage, so I had to maintain the tactical advantage.

* * *

I MADE my primary lookout in the boat's wheelhouse. It was dry and offered protection on three sides with a partial fourth. It also offered several broken spaces on both port and starboard sides to observe and shoot from, if necessary. If a firefight did occur, I could lower myself into the cargo hold, which was dry and had thicker walls to offer more protection. I placed all the scuba gear down there along the starboard wall facing shore, where there was a break in the rebar and cement large enough for an adult to squeeze through and drop down into the water to escape. I included the gear I purchased for Marcy as well. I laid up the Kevlar blanket and all the extra food and water behind a pile of rubble that offered another barrier of protection if needed. Along the port-hull-wall was the rubber raft which I left by the largest gap. It would just need a shove to drop down a few feet into the water.

Back up in the wheelhouse, the sun came out from behind cloud cover long enough to drive the rain away as a last act before it set for the night. Inside the broken wheelhouse, I tried to make myself comfortable. I laid out the sleeping bag, ate some beef jerky, and forced myself to drink water. I knew staying alert was important, but MS-13 was just getting directions, and it would be a while before they could get their logistical act together. The breeze was warm, and the boat was immovable, but it was the sound of ocean waves a few feet below that lulled me to sleep.

Around midnight I heard what sounded like a faint buzzing noise. I knew better than to shirk it off. The night vision attached to the helmet Drake sent me was a PVS-14, a cutting-edge piece of tech that allowed the user to see like it was midday. I grabbed the helmet and dropped the night vision. It took only a few seconds to locate a large quad drone flying over the boats a couple of hundred yards north. It stopped over the large gap in the two sections of boats. The exact location I had given as the first dive spot.

After hovering for ten seconds, the drone did the most amazing thing. It lowered down to just a few feet over the water, flipped over, and splashed down on the water's surface. A moment later, it submerged. I watched in awe as bubbles floated to the surface, praying the drone wasn't outfitted with cutting torches or any other type of robotic tools that would allow it to snag the drugs. After ten minutes, it popped back up to the surface right side up. The rotors started up, and it proceeded to rise into the air without the drugs. The drone continued down the line of boats at about thirty feet heading in my direction.

I had no idea that drones could go from air to underwater, but I did know they had thermal scans, and scrambled to push my few pieces of gear down into the hold of the boat and jumped down after. My hope was the thick hull of the old ship would block any thermal imaging the drone might have. I also hid under the Kevlar blanket and made sure not to move. The buzzing passed by and continued out of range. It was a good two minutes before I got up from under the blanket. The cost of that drone must have been astronomical. My stomach tightened as a reminder I was in way over my head. I looked out a small break in the concrete to make sure the drone was nowhere in sight. I prayed I hadn't been flagged on a thermal scan and contemplated moving to a different boat, but it would take too long to reposition my gear, and another drone could show up at any time.

Using the secure satellite phone, I texted Drake to check in on his status but received no response. Still, I texted him the rough outline of my plan and my location just in case he could do something, anything. Annie texted me on the other phone to ask for an update. I gripped the phone, wishing the device was her hand intertwined with mine. I texted back that I'd know more in the morning and that I loved her and to kiss the girls goodnight for me. She asked where I was sleeping, and I just replied: *Somewhere safe*. I deleted all her texts just in case the phone fell into the wrong hands, but I knew that would not be enough. If everything failed, I hoped to have time to toss the phones into the seawater before the end, thus destroying them permanently. For security purposes, I stayed down in the cargo hold for the rest of the night. Between the cool temperature and the sound of the waves slapping against the hull of the boat, it was quite comfortable in the eight-decade-old cargo hold. However, I slept very little.

* * *

THE NEXT MORNING, I awoke to seagulls squawking in a nest above the wheelhouse. They seemed to be in the middle of a family argument about the new tenant who moved in beneath them the day before. The sun rose a short while later in a glorious golden fireball. Looking out the break in the hull, I was glad to see rough water, as it would keep the boaters, kayakers, and anglers away from my location.

I purchased a solar charger for the cell phones which I kept plugged in. Annie texted to ask how things were going. I told her that I had been doing some dives and that Drake was heading here with his team to take over. All of which was true, but from a ten-thousand-foot point of view. I reminded her to have Dad place an order for #2 diesel for the tractors. With nothing left to do but wait, I settled back into my rubber raft and sleeping bag and tried to rest in the cargo hold.

* * *

A FEW HOURS LATER, the seas had calmed, and the sun was high in a clear blue sky. I made my way back up to the wheelhouse with minimal gear. The chest rig, helmet, shotgun, AR-10, along with some water and beef jerky. A few kayakers paddled along the shore about a half mile away. Were it any other day, I would have loved to be on shore with my family, playing in the water, or fishing nearby. I texted JT to check in from his end. He texted back that he had not heard anything further and that he created software bots to scan the Internet, and dark web, for anyone searching for my name, but so far, nothing had come up. I thanked him again for his help. With nothing more to do, I went back down into the ship's hold, lay on the rubber raft, and tried to rest some more. Had the concrete boats been in better shape, I could have seen Amber talking about repurposing them into VRBO rental units. Besides the dull sound of the waves outside, there was a faint drip from somewhere inside the hull, which had a soothing effect. A warm sea breeze flowed through the darkened space and kept the area comfortable. Gosh, I hated waiting. Whether it was a root canal or a firefight with the world's most notorious gang, if there was something miserable to do, I wanted to get it over with as soon as possible.

I ate a sparse lunch of beef jerky, a PowerBar, and water. My last thoughts before drifting off to a nap were of the cement boats themselves. If only they could talk. Who were the men transported on them during World War II? What were their stories? Who did, and did not, return from Europe and the Pacific? Were there any men transported on them who were still alive? What was it like to live during the 1940s, a time when the entire country pulled together? Men, women, and children collected scrap metal, and when that wasn't enough, people thought outside the box and came up with ideas like building transport ships out of concrete. It was a time of sacrifice but also a time of ingenuity and hope.

Today's world seemed to be the polar opposite. We had all but driven God from the public sector. Politics had infiltrated everything from education to medicine and science, and we seemed to be reaping what we sowed. The country hadn't been this divided since 1860. Like Rome, we were a world empire overflowing with hubris who thought they would last forever but seemed to be on borrowed time.

AROUND FOUR O'CLOCK in the afternoon, I awoke both confused and disoriented. It took a good twenty seconds to get my bearings. I texted Drake to check in again but received no response. Where was my friend and mentor? Knowing how quickly a drone was sent out to scope the location, I knew in my gut that MS-13 wasn't going to let another night go by without getting their drugs. It was coming up to game time. I started to position gear in place for a worst-case scenario confrontation. I'd start in the wheelhouse with just what I could carry. The helmet and night vision, AR-10, and four spare mags in my chest rig. Down in the hull, I repositioned all the scuba gear near the crawl space on the starboard side facing the beach where we could exit. There was nothing else to do except wait.

SIXTEEN

Night came on the Chesapeake Bay like the unfurling of a curtain. It was a quick but gorgeous, fiery sunset. Clouds moved in to cover the moon and all but a few stars. A boom of thunder in the distance reminded me of the tuxedo-clad announcer at professional boxing matches who shouted, *Let's get ready to rumble.* It was as if the heavens knew something big was about to go down. Was there a possibility this could go smoothly? Even if I got Marcy in exchange for the drugs, this organization was pure evil and would never stop until they exacted their vengeance. The chances of either me or Marcy coming out of this alive were minuscule. Still, I somehow knew this was where I was meant to be.

With the arrival of darkness, I changed from shorts back into my wetsuit. I removed the small outboard off the stern of the rubber raft and paddled out a few hundred yards from the boat. I anchored the dingy using a chunk of concrete I found in the hull and a piece of black paracord. Just enough to keep it in place. With my wetsuit, mask, snorkel, and fins on, I swam back, unfurling another line of weighted paracord I had attached to the raft. The line would sit far enough below the waterline to not get caught in any boat prop that might go by. The dinghy was what I'd use to pull Marcy in if the exchange went smoothly.

* * *

BACK INSIDE THE hull of the boat, I kept the wetsuit on and wore the battle gear over it. My thoughts drifted to my new friend Charles Coyne. The bow-tie-wearing coffee friend who believed I was sent as an answer to his prayer. He would belly laugh seeing me decked out like a Navy SEAL in a wetsuit with a chest rig, helmet, and battle rifle in hand. He'd give me an *I told you so* in his Cajun drawl. The image vanished. Replaced by self-centered fearful thoughts of self-preservation. Of all the ways of dying, I never thought it would happen alone on a half-sunken World War II boat in the Chesapeake Bay, yet here I was. Alone, hundreds of miles from my family in the dark of night, about to face off against one of the most vile organizations on the planet.

No, I was never alone, I reminded myself.

I spoke Hebrews 13:5 out loud again as a reminder. "I will never leave thee, nor forsake thee." I refused to pray for my safety. I was in His hands, and like Christ said, "Not My will but Your will be done." I did ask for strength for what lay ahead and received an immediate response as the knot in my stomach unwound for the first time since I had landed on the boat. I shifted the prayer from me to Marcy. "Please, Lord, watch over her. She doesn't know you yet."

* * *

It was around ten o'clock when the fast boat showed up. It was flat, black, and had no running lights. It pulled right up to the spot I had given for the first drop. The spot the drone had explored underwater. I texted JT to let him know it was game time and told him to continue to give directions even if our communications went out. A spotlight from the fast boat ran all along the half-sunken World War II boats for a few minutes before two drones rose from the fast boat's deck. Each flew in opposite directions, down the line of boats. I dropped down into the cargo hold and continued to watch through a break in the portside as one of the drones whizzed by.

A diver came out of the fast boat's cabin and plopped over the side as a driver maintained the boat controls. I could tell by the figure's outline it was a young male. I swapped out the night vision and looked through the scope of the AR-10. It was Jeremy. He was dressed in all black and had an AR-style rifle slung over his back.

"You fool," I whispered.

After a few minutes, the diver resurfaced. The next move would be for them to deposit more cryptocurrency into the account JT had set up to receive the combination to the underwater lock. A moment later, my first cell phone went dead. Someone was using a high-tech jamming device.

I scanned back and forth and couldn't find the drones. A moment later, I picked up the hull of a twenty-five-foot Defender Class Coast Guard boat as it appeared from the darkness behind the fast boat. Its bright orange foam-filled collar is unmistakable from any other craft. It only had a couple of running lights on and seemed to have snuck up on the drug boat. There was a big fat fifty-caliber canon on deck with a sailor standing behind it. I nearly shouted with excitement.

Drake had received my message and called in the cavalry. This could not have been more providential.

"Well done, Drake," I whispered.

The Coast Guard Defender crept up behind the fast boat. I waited for some petty officer to shout over a loudspeaker to lower their guns or shut the boat off, but nothing happened. There was a brief exchange of voices between the two boats, but nothing that seemed confrontational. If anything, the voices sounded friendly.

"Dear Lord, no," I said, realizing the Coast Guard was there to help oversee the deal.

Marcy was right again. There was, in fact, a faction of the Coast Guard who were compromised. The Coast Guard boat ran a spotlight up and down the hulls of the World War II boats clearly checking for snipers. I ducked down and retrieved the second throwaway phone I had purchased. This satellite phone I kept wrapped in a Mylar bag for protection and prayed it still worked. It did. I texted JT and told him to go to phase two once he got the second batch of crypto. He received confirmation and passed along the combination to the underwater lock. I watched as the diver dropped back over the side of the fast boat. I moved back to the break in the port hull, I zeroed in on Jeremy with the AR scope. The idiot sat at the helm and spoke from time to time to someone still in the cuddy cabin, who I assumed was in control of the drones. Was Marcy with them, though? Ten minutes later, the diver surfaced with the case of drugs. I pinged JT to let him know phase one was complete.

JT informed them the girl was to be released next, and I would give them the location for the next drop of drugs. Once they confirmed the drugs were there, I would give them the combination in exchange for the last deposit of crypto.

They countered with: *Girl only for the second load.*

I had JT agree to the last-minute modification but say they needed to show proof of life first. A picture was sent via the dark web messenger with a time stamp. JT responded that it was not good enough, and we had a drone circling them at their current location. It was a lie of course. Marcy was brought to the deck of the Coast Guard boat. I was surprised she wasn't on the fast boat, but it just reaffirmed how dirty these sailors were. From what I could see, she looked to be intact and relatively healthy. She struggled against the sailor holding her, which was a good sign. I recognized the Coast Guardsman as one of the two who stopped me outside Cox's property the day I was in the kayak. I shifted the rifle to the helm. Even behind the wheelhouse's glass, I confirmed it was the second male with the first Coast Guardsman that day. A moment later, the sailor pulled Marcy back into the wheelhouse. I had JT relay the location of the drugs. The fast boat moved off toward my direction and passed by within five feet of the break in the hull. I could have easily picked off Jeremy and jumped on board had Marcy been on that boat. The Coast Guard Defender followed from a distance but picked up on the rubber raft floating nearby. They stopped and scanned their spotlight over the raft, then to the World War II boats nearest the dinghy.

The fast boat reached the second dive spot at the end of the line and idled its engine. The diver went over again and, five minutes later, was back on the surface. The reality was that if they brought an underwater torch, they could cut through the chain and lock, but it would take time, and they needed to disappear quick.

Marcy was brought from the center cabin of the Coast Guard boat to the bow. They were a hundred yards off the portside of my location. This was it. The most dangerous part of the mission.

JT told them to release the girl into the floating dingy off the side of boat eight, where she would *wait for pick up*. A complete bluff, but the more details we added, the better. There were words exchanged between the sailor and Marcy, and she was thrown over the side of the Coast Guard boat into the water. I wanted to open fire on the sailor who did this, but I waited and watched as Marcy swam through the choppy surf toward the rubber raft. Once she was on board the rubber raft, I had JT relay the combination to the underwater lock. All our cards were on the table now.

The diver went back down, and the Coast Guard boat stayed near Marcy and the dingy. The sailor on board the Coast Guard boat held his position on the deck behind the fifty caliber. I had no more bargaining power other than the time for them to get the drugs to the surface, open the case, and verify the drugs were real. The moment it was confirmed, they would kill Marcy.

I found the end of the submerged paracord and pulled it hand over hand toward me. Through a crack in the hull, I could see Marcy untie the anchor line, which allowed the raft to move quicker. Even in her condition, she figured out what was happening and knew enough to drop the anchor line. The diver was still underwater next to the fast boat. Suddenly, a flood light snapped on Marcy from the Coast Guard boat as she moved toward the break in the hull where I pulled from. I was still hidden from sight, as was the paracord rope, but how I wished there was just one more soldier to back me up. Someone who could shoot the Coast Guard's light out. I prayed no one would open fire on Marcy while she was this exposed. Down the line, the diver was still underwater, but I had to hurry. Marcy made it to the break in the side of the cargo hold just as the diver broke the surface with the second load of drugs.

I heard him spit out his regulator and say the words, "I got it."

"Marcy, jump and swim out to me!" I shouted from the darkness.

She didn't hesitate, she jumped into the water and swam the last few yards. She crawled over rubble and through the gap in the hull and fell into my arms, sobbing.

A moment later, I heard the faint words, "Confirmed."

Concrete exploded behind us on the starboard hull side. I forgot about the drones. They were armed! Another drone lowered down on the portside near us and started firing. Just outside, the rubber dinghy deflated. I pulled Marcy back into the bowels of the hull behind the pile of rubble and covered her under the Kevlar blanket. I dropped the night vision down and grabbed the twelve-gauge. My first two shots were slugs, the rest were double 00 bucks. I blasted the closest drone out the starboard side in one shot. It blew apart into bits of plastic and metal. The drone on the portside entered the gap in the hull where Marcy had just crawled in. It hovered inside like some science fiction probe before it randomly started to fire off rounds from its onboard gun. I racked and blasted until the shotgun was empty. The drone fell, damaged but continued to fire and rotate around on the ground, spraying bullets. I ducked behind the rubble pile as the damaged drone spun like an eggbeater on steroids. I shouldered the AR-10 and emptied a full magazine into the drone until it stopped. I changed mags and rushed to the portside opening to face the Coast Guard Defender.

To my left, the fast boat had started up, and Jeremy and another male were firing automatic rifles in my direction. I was out of range and fired off a few bursts to let them know not to come any closer. Hopefully, they'd back off and simply try to get away. Then big brother stepped in. The Coast Guard Defender opened up with the fifty cal. There was a flash from the deck. I had a split second to dive down before a large piece of concrete blew apart where my head had just been. Another blast opened a hole at the waterline, allowing seawater to start to enter in.

I crawled back over to Marcy as more shots from the fifty caliber followed. Mortar and stone exploded around us, and the World War II boat shuddered like she was going to sink. Once behind the pile of rubble, I crawled under the Kevlar blanket with Marcy. Even before I turned on my penlight, I could tell she was crying.

I forced a smile. "Nice pickle we're in, huh?"

"Please take me home, Brandon."

I cradled her head against my chest and didn't respond. Her home was in cinders. Her mother and father were both dead. Her elderly grandfather was a mess. This poor girl had no hope and no spiritual protection. I wanted to weep for her.

Bullets ricocheted all around us. One hit my foot, with only minimal pain. Had it not lost velocity penetrating the hull before it went through the rubble pile and hit the Kevlar blanket, it might have torn my foot clean off. I made sure both our heads were as low as possible. The Coast Guard boat was in no rush to leave.

They were going to unload on us until they were sure we were both dead.

Our only chance was to get the scuba tank and retreat out the starboard side and into the safety of the sea. Swim underwater to the beach and escape. The World War II boats would offer us a barrier of protection from the Defender. The gear was only a few feet from us, but we'd have to stand up to access both the gear and crawl space. I wondered if Marcy knew how to buddy breath, let alone use a regulator. The gunfire ceased all of a sudden. The only thing I could hear besides the ringing in my ears was the rumble of the fast boat's engines. They hadn't left yet. What were they waiting for?

Voices. There were voices getting closer. They were coming onto the boat to make sure we were dead. I moved out from the blanket and slid along the wet floor to look out several new gaps in the portside of the hull. Beyond the boats in the distance, there was something in the moonlight. It was nothing but a blurry spot at first, but it grew into the shape of a plane. No, a biplane. No one seemed to hear it or see it yet besides me.

"Luke, you old fool, what're you doing," I whispered.

The plane slowed down and flew in low like it was going to land. Just as it passed over the fast boat, Luke dropped what appeared to be a Molotov cocktail the size of a whiskey jug onto the deck of the fast boat. The flames exploded and one man caught on fire. He screamed in pain and jumped overboard while two others pulled out fire extinguishers. The floating Coast Guard boat came to life again. It fired one single volley from its deck canon. A moment later, the only sound was the putter of the biplane's damaged engine as it trailed off toward shore with its wings struggling to stay level. I rushed over to the starboard side of the hull. Through a break, I could see the plane pitch to the left and run parallel to the shore. It crashed in the shallows near the beach. There was movement from the cockpit, which told me Luke was alive.

I turned back around and took aim with the AR-10 but decided not to fire on the Coast Guard boat. We were overpowered and outgunned. Maybe if I went quiet, they'd assume we were dead? I retreated behind the rubble and under the blanket with Marcy.

"What's happening?"

"Grampy showed up thinking he's the cavalry," I said. "Stubborn old coot flew over in his biplane. Coast Guard shot him down."

"Is he dead? Brandon, is he dead?"

"I think he's okay. The plane splashed down in the water near the shore. It didn't look like it landed hard."

"What are we going to do?"

"When I give the word, get up, put on a scuba mask behind you, and jump out the gap behind you into the water. We're gonna do what's called buddy breathing with a scuba tank and swim underwater toward shore. Do you understand?"

"I know what buddy breathing is, but I've never done it."

"Just breath normal," I said. "I'll put on the tank, which has two regulators. Whatever happens, do not surface. The water is our friend and our protection. We gotta go pretty deep, though."

Suddenly, I heard the revving of the fast boat's engines. They were leaving. I crawled back to the port-side break and peered out. The Coast Guard boat was still in position. Both sailors were on deck. One of them had night vision, while the other stood behind the deck canon. The fifty cal flashed, and I turned to crawl back. The hull exploded behind me, and I was hit with pieces of rebar and stone, most of which was absorbed by my plated vest and helmet. Some cut into the back of my legs and neck. My adrenaline was pumping too much to feel pain at this point. I made it back behind the rubble pile and tossed both cell phones out the side and into the water. Marcy gave me a look as if she knew what I was doing.

I prayed out loud. "Father, I ask for a miracle where one is not deserved—"

"Deus ex machina," Marcy said in a panic-stricken voice as she lifted the blanket for me to crawl under.

"What?"

"Deus ex machina," she said. "It means God out of the machine."

I turned to her, shocked. "Seriously. You're quoting Greek at a time like this?"

The fifty cal blew another hole in the side of the boat. More rubble and rebar sprayed around us, and my ears pulsed from the sounds.

"It's Latin," she shouted, half serious and half crying. "The cavalry is what you're praying for from God. A mathematical impossibility at this point. In the movies, when help rushes in on the third act that has not been introduced previously, it ruins the movie, and the audience cries foul. Face it, we're gonna die, Brandon!"

"I've been in worse fixes."

"Bull."

"I'm not joking," I said. "I have. Granted, I'm scared too."

"I don't want to go back with them."

"It will be over my dead body," I said.

Another explosion rocked the boat. The Kevlar

blanket shivered as fragments of cement hit it. I needed time to get us into the water, and they weren't giving it to us. There were now massive holes in the portside. I rolled out flat and started to fire back toward the Coast Guard boat. I fired until the magazine was empty. During the exchange, I knocked out their spotlight but didn't think I hit anyone.

In between changing mags, I shouted over my shoulder. "Get into the water and swim."

"No, I—"

"Swim! Get to your grandfather. I'll hold them off and be right behind you." Marcy didn't respond, so I jacked my tone up. "Move! Now!"

She slithered out from the blanket. I turned and unloaded as fast as my finger would pull the trigger. It was doubtful I hit any targets; I just wanted them to stop firing long enough for Marcy to get into the water. The starboard hull of the World War II boat would offer her protection on her swim to shore. I fell back behind the pile of rubble to reload another mag. Marcy was still there. I expected to see a frightened deer. A young girl frozen in panic. Instead, I saw a teary-eyed teen who looked worried about me. All this I read in her eyes.

"You drive me nuts," I said.

"I've lost everyone," she said, crying. "I won't leave."

"Here," I said, handing her the Glock. "There's no safety on this."

"I've never—"

"Keep it pointed away from either of us and your finger off the trigger until you want to shoot. If something happens to me and a bad man shows up, just point and shoot."

There was a buzzing noise in the distance. It was hard to hear over the ringing in my ears. The thumping of a helicopter came into focus. The Coast Guard's fifty cal restarted, which washed out any, and all, background noise. I gripped Marcy's head tight to my chest, expecting to be blown into eternity as we hunkered down behind the pile of rubble. My heart sank. The Coast Guard had called in air support. I had somehow foolishly convinced myself that God wasn't going to let Marcy die in her sins without knowing Him. What arrogance on my part. My thoughts went to Annie, Amber, and Emily. Then to my son, Jonah.

"Daddy will see you soon," I whispered.

SEVENTEEN

THERE WAS THE SWISH, WHICH I KNEW FROM MY TIME IN the military, was the sound of a rocket being launched. I shut my eyes and held Marcy tight. Everything slowed down. I could feel my heart pound beneath the thick chest plate, which was strong enough to stop a 5.56 NATO rifle round. The rocket would cut through it like nothing, and there would be nothing left to identify either of us. I prayed Drake would claim my body so Annie would not have to. A moment later, there was an explosion. The sound was deafening.

Marcy screamed over and over. "Make it stop! Make it stop!"

"Don't fear, Marcy. Close your eyes and believe in Jesus." With my last breath, I was going to use it to preach to this girl.

Two things happened. First, I realized we weren't dead. Second, the gunfire went silent. It was replaced by the crackle of fire and the rhythmic thumping of helicopter rotors. I got up from behind the debris pile. By this time, the entire portside of the boat was exposed to the sea with water washing in and out. To my left, the fast boat was on fire. What looked like two charred corpses were hunched over what little remained of the hull of the boat. Waves fought against the flames in a battle in which water would soon win.

Above, an MH-6 Little Bird chopper hovered in place. A massive light flashed on from its nose to scan back and forth before stopping at the gap where I stood. I waved to whomever it was in the chopper, assuming they were *friendly*. Even at a couple of hundred yards, I could feel the heat from what was left of the fast boat. A moment later, the boat broke apart and the bodies disappeared. All I could think about were Jeremy's parents. As much as a lowlife scumbag drug dealer as he was, there were going to be grieving parents, and my heart broke for them.

The chopper moved over the deck of the Coast Guard Defender. The boat was riddled with bullets, and the glass on the center console cabin was shattered. Two sailors were on deck with their arms up. One heavily armed soldier repelled down from the chopper onto the deck of the Coast Guard boat. In moments, the sailor's hands were zip cuffed. Through the chopper's spotlight, I confirmed it was the two Coast Guardsmen I met outside Cox's estate. I hoped the corruption didn't run deeper into the Coast Guard than those two. The chopper moved closer to me. A diver with a mask and snorkel dropped into the water and swam over. He surfaced, carrying a light chest rig and a short stock rifle I didn't recognize. He put his mask on his forearm and clipped his fins to his chest rig. The blond hair and beard I did recognize.

"Boss Man, that you?" John Homer said, crawling into

the hull of the old ship. "Man, you look ugly without your beard."

"Will you shut up with the Boss Man stuff," I said, referring to the nickname John Homer and his partner Jose Paronto gave me during our last job together. I hugged the muscle-bound man. John Homer, former Navy SEAL and one of the newest employees for my government friend Roger Drake's off-the-books team.

"Boy, you really step in it, Hall," Homer said, turning semiserious. "You turn down Drake's job only to take on the entire MS-13 cartel from South America."

"Marcy, you can come out now," I said.

Marcy crawled out from behind the rubble pile and rushed to my side.

"Marcy, I'd like you to meet my friend. Deus ex machina."

"What's that?" Homer asked, shaking her hand.

"I'll explain later," I said.

Homer scanned the scene. The broken drones, the shards of rubble, and the exposed hull of the ship. "How are you two still alive?"

I pointed up. "I prayed that God wouldn't let harm come to this young lady until she knew Him."

Homer shook his head. "I hope you realize that you're a walking miracle, young lady." He turned to me. "We got a lot of cleanup to do by morning."

"Luke," I said, remembering the biplane.

"Grampy," Marcy repeated.

"Who?" Homer said, his head flipping back and forth between us.

"Never mind," I said, pointing out the starboard side toward shore where a half-submerged biplane sat. "We gotta get to shore quick."

"What in the name of Teddy Roosevelt is that—"

Homer said. "A biplane? Boss Man, you get yourself into the weirdest situations."

I grabbed my emergency first aid kit. "Come on. Let's swim over and check on Luke."

"I'm coming," Marcy said, starting to put on the fins and mask I got her.

It was a ten-minute swim to the plane where we found Luke alive but too exhausted to crawl out of the wreckage.

"Grampy, you knucklehead!" Marcy shouted from the half-submerged wing.

Luke smiled with a bandage still on his head. "Hi, sweetie. Boy, did I miss you."

We helped Luke out, and the four of us walked onto shore.

"I'll get him to the truck," I said, half-carrying Luke. "I'm parked just down the road."

"We have the local sheriff at the park entrance standing guard," Homer said. "I'll have someone notify him to bring you to your vehicle."

"My gear?" I said.

"I'll pick up your gear and get it back to where it belongs."

I pointed to the distance where the flaming fast boat, Coast Guard Defender, and a hovering helicopter were situated just beyond the sunken World War II boats. It looked like a scene from a post-apocalyptic sci-fi movie. Old-world technology juxtaposed against new high-tech machinery. In my opinion, the newer military chopper and Coast Guard boat were still outclassed by the old-school navy boats.

"And what about that mess?"

"Drake has a Navy boat coming out of Norfolk to commandeer the Coast Guard Defender. Until we know how deep MS-13 infiltrated that Coast Guard base, we're handing it off to the Navy." Homer started back into the shallows. "This entire debacle will probably go down as a training exercise gone wrong. It's bad PR all around." A moment later, Homer put on his mask, dropped below the surface of the water, and disappeared.

* * *

LATER THAT NIGHT, I called Annie and JT to let them know I was fine and would be home in twenty-four hours. The next morning, Annie called to tell me she saw a coincidental headline on the news about a Coast Guard training exercise explosion off of Kiptopeke State Park.

"I had nothing to do with that boat exploding."

"I'm wise to the way you phrase things to get out of lying, my love," Annie said. "Suffice it to say you were in the proximity when the boating accident did occur?"

"Define proximity?"

"Brandon Hall!"

"I really can't talk over unsecured lines, honey. There's a rumor that Drake's team came in to clean up some corruption. I'll explain later. I'm fine, though. Marcy is fine. Luke is fine. Everything is fine. God is good."

"Well, I want a more formal debrief when you get home."

"I promise to fill you in on all the details."

Annie giggled. "Looking forward to it."

My next phone call was to Roger Drake.

He didn't even say hello. "Boy, you really stepped into it this time."

"Good to hear from you, too," I said.

"All I gotta say is the Lord ain't done with you yet, but that doesn't mean you go picking fights with the biggest bad guys on the planet without me, you hear?"

"Loud and clear," I said.

"I practically had to hijack a C-130 to get the team back here to help you. I can't tell you how many favors I had to call in to save your skin."

"So, I need another favor."

Drake laughed. "You are one bold son of a gun, but that's one of the things I love about you."

"What do I do with this crypto?"

"What do you mean?"

"What do you mean what do I mean? I finagled, like, $100,000 in some random crypto currency from MS-13?"

"This was all off the books," Drake said. "We're almost done scrubbing the entire event as well. It's found money. You couldn't give it to the government if you wanted to at this point. It's yours."

I thought for a minute. "What can the team use it for?"

"A lot of things," he said. "This new admin is trying to defund groups like mine, and after what happened with Homer and his wife, I want to buy a piece of property and build Bridgett, Paronto, and Homer a couple of simple prefab homes on it. Nothing fancy, but I want them off-the-grid and away from DC where I can protect them better. I want them near me."

"Then take it."

"You sure?"

"I'm sure. It's not much, but it will give you a down payment for your project."

"That's generous of you, Brandon."

"I have my daily bread," I said. "I trust you implicitly,

Roger. Besides, I wouldn't know my elbow from Bite-Coin."

"It's Bitcoin, not Bite-Coin, you ninny."

"I'll have my buddy relay the crypto wallet code thingy to you," I said. "I can't believe we are at the point where you have to almost self-fund your group."

"Not just yet," Drake said. "However, we do need to put in place firewalls to make sure my guys are protected. Times are changing, son, and it's getting harder and harder to tell the good guys from the bad guys. For now, I'm operating within the boundaries of the country, but I need to prepare for a day when the government goes off the reservation in regard to the Constitution."

"What's your prediction?"

"Christ returns. We win." Drake paused for a moment. "Between now and then, it's a crapshoot. Civil War may be coming, or the US could end up Balkanizing with redoubt states and communist states and end up a country in name only."

"You think that could happen?"

"Look at your license to conceal carry a firearm. It's reciprocal in dozens of other states, but not all of them."

"Yeah."

"That's completely unconstitutional, yet it's accepted as normal. You may end up seeing credit cards and driver's licenses operate with the same restrictions."

"Seriously?"

"Already, certain rental car companies won't recognize out-of-state licenses. State lawmakers in certain states like California are being banned from visiting other states."

"You're making me nervous."

"Sorry," Drake said. "It's not my intent. Don't fear, as

the good book says over and over, my brother. Just know that God's in control, and I'm always keeping an eye on you from afar."

"One of the reasons why I love you, old man."

"Who you calling old? Speak for yourself."

"Say hi to the rest of the team for me."

"Will do, son."

* * *

LATER THAT MORNING, we buried Cassie in the family cemetery plot on Luke's farm. Pastor Bob conducted the service. Luke, Marcy, Pastor Bob, and his wife were the only ones in attendance. After the service, we had a light lunch at Luke's. I loosened my tie and was more than ready to go home. However, I would miss these new friends. Luke Seabold was a solid man, and Marcy had a bright future ahead of her. I wanted to say something prolific before I left. Something about God that would stick with her. Instead, I drew a blank. At sixteen, Marcy was already smarter than me. Instead, I shook Luke's hand and hugged Marcy. For long moments Marcy wouldn't let go. She burst into tears, and I followed.

I simply said. "I love you guys."

"Please stay in touch," Marcy said.

"I promise."

"I'll never forget what you did for me, Brandon."

I pointed up. "Use that brilliant mind of yours and do the math. Our rescue wasn't me, but divine intervention. You realize that now, don't you?"

After a long pause, Marcy nodded.

* * *

Before leaving town, I drove by the coffee shop. I ordered my iced coffee and wandered up the stairs to the second floor. My new friend Charles Coyne wasn't in his usual spot with his face in the Bible. Will, the owner, came up the stairs with a tray of crystal glasses which he started to place on a decorated table to prepare for some fancy event.

"I'm gonna miss this place," I said.

"All rested up from your vacation?"

I chuckled. "Let's just say I'm ready to go home."

"Sorry to see you go."

"Say, I was wondering if Charles Coyne had been in today?"

Will placed another crystal glass down. "Who?"

"The older gentleman who sat upstairs. Wore a different bow tie each day?"

Will's face didn't change as he continued to arrange glasses in a fancy pattern. I added, "Short-cropped gray hair? Handsome fella? Tall?"

Will shook his head. "Don't know who you're talking about."

"The old guy with the Cajun-Creole accent who dressed like he stepped from a silent film from the 1920s?"

Will said, "I know all my regulars, and he doesn't jump out at me."

As if on cue, I watched Will say hello to several customers by first name as they passed by. Maybe Will missed one of his regulars, or maybe I had imagined meeting Charles Coyne? No, Emily and my family had met him too. The entire drive home, I thought of Charles, wondering if I would meet this mysterious man again.

EPILOGUE

THE REUNION BACK AT THE FARM FELT LIKE NOTHING I had ever experienced before. I had mentally resided myself to a horrific death by firefight alone on the water in the middle of the night, but there I was, back on my farm, embracing my family and alive. I never wanted to leave home again. Maybe this was a scintilla of what Lazarus felt like coming back from the dead. I would fill Annie in on the entire story of what happened when the time was right. For now, I just wanted to be near my family, manage the herd, tinker with my old tractors, walk over to Mom and Dad's cabin for Sunday dinner, and simply relax for the next forty or fifty years.

AFTER A SHOWER AND HOT MEAL, I found Amber in her apartment painting with a handkerchief wrapped over her auburn hair. I had to come clean with her about what I'd seen in Cape Charles. About seeing her fiancé, Steve, meeting with her cousin's employee. There was no doubt they were playing her. I decided to talk to her about marriage in general before revealing my observations. She had been traumatized by both her parents' horrific deaths as well as her brother's murder. Telling her that her fiancé might be manipulating her to get at her inheritance could push her back a few steps.

"You got a sec?"

"Sure," she said.

"Something about Steve we need to talk about." She stopped painting. "First off, I'm not your dad, and I don't want you to think I'm telling you what to do." I paused, not sure how to wade into a conversation with a young lady who was not my biological daughter. Emily was nowhere near dating age yet, let alone marriage, so this was all new to me.

"Spit it out, Brandon," she said, continuing to paint.

"I don't want to see you rush into something you might regret."

"What makes you say that?"

"I just, uhm, think you guys are a little young."

"Anything else?"

"Steve gave me a bad feeling."

"I don't think you've even met him?"

"Well, I er, um. I just got a bad vibe in my gut and—"

"Anything else you're not telling me?" Amber repeated, her free hand on her hip.

"Like?"

"Like my cousin, Ricky, paid him to woo me?"

My jaw dropped. "How'd—"

"I'm no dunce, Brandon. Do you think I couldn't hack his accounts? The idiot's phone password was literally one, two, three, four, five, six."

"So, the wedding is off?"

"Yes, I gave the ring back."

I exhaled for a good ten seconds before finding a chair to sit down in. I told her about seeing Steve in Cape Charles with her cousin's employee.

"It took me a while to catch on," she said, "but once I hacked Steve's email, I knew what he was up to. My cousin is desperate for money. He's such a scumbag."

"Are you sure you're gonna be okay?"

She waved her hand as if it were no big deal. "It was a gaudy ring anyway."

"That's not what I mean, Amber. You've been through so much in the past few years."

"I'll be fine. I have my family," she said, giving me a forced smile and wink, but her eyes had a tinge of moisture to them.

"You always have us, even when you do get married one day."

"Thanks, Brandon. I've already decided I want a nice small wedding here on the farm."

"I'd like that," I said. "It's good for the farm."

WALKING BACK TO THE FARMHOUSE, I said a silent prayer of thanks for Amber's progress. A blow like that six months prior would have sent her into a mental fetal position. It had been such a long road for her to get to where she was. Yet here she was, stronger than ever and turning into the woman God meant her to be. I was excited to see what He had in store for her future.

Just before I entered the house, Drake texted me with a message: *I got a perfect summer side job for you. Stay cool in Alaska?* I didn't respond. Instead, I put my cell away and went inside. Annie and Emily were watching our favorite movie, *It's a Wonderful Life*. It was the part where

Clarence Odbody was trying to convince George Bailey he was an angel. I snuggled in between them. A short while later, Amber joined us with a bowl of popcorn. I turned up the volume, which allowed me to turn down the world outside.

"Look, Daddy," Emily said. "Clarence has a tie just like your friend, Mr. Coyne."

IF YOU LIKE THIS, YOU MAY ALSO ENJOY: TRUTH IN THE NAME

A POLITICAL THRILLER BY F.D. ADKINS

What if someone erased your memory? Would you still know God?

President Denali's war on crime has eliminated most criminals, but not all.

When he goes after the rest, he creates his own personal army. But at what cost?

Ellie Hatcher is tapped for a role in this secretive sect. She must leave all behind in less than 24 hours and she can't even tell her parents. With the guilt eating at her, she decides to go and serve her nation.

But something's not right. People are losing their memories and their will to disagree. Except for Ellie.

As the truth is revealed, Ellie enters a race against time to save the world and the man she's falling in love with from the president's thirst for more power.

Ellie Hatcher may have been chosen as a pawn by the president, but her presence in the training facility just might be a special assignment from God.

AVAILABLE NOW

ABOUT THE AUTHOR

John Theo Jr. received a bachelor's degree in psychology from Salem State University, and an M.F.A. in Creative Writing from Pine Manor College in Chestnut Hill, Massachusetts. For almost two decades his diverse writing portfolio included roles as a movie critic, a magazine freelance writer, and a college professor where he taught screenwriting.

John grew up in the suburbs north of Boston where much of his youth was spent buried under stacks of comic books. He latched onto any story involving far off places and fantastical characters. Years later he realized the novels and movies that impacted him on the deepest level were ones with a spiritual component. In hindsight, he realized that his youthful obsession with these stories was, in fact, a longing for the Divine.

Today, John Theo Jr. writes novels from a Christian perspective. Like the stories of his youth, John enjoys tales with an otherworldly component to them as well as a good measure of action, adventure, and romance.

Made in the USA
Middletown, DE
20 January 2023